The Silver Bestiary

Also by A.R. McHugh

Saccades

The Tales of Cupid and Psyche

The Silver Bestiary

A.R. McHugh

The right of A.R. McHugh to be identified as the author of this work
has been asserted in accordance with the Copyright Act 1968.
ISBN: 978-0-6489145-7-0
This edition published in Australia in 2022 by Diving Bell, an imprint
of Diving Bell Education. www.divingbelleducation.com

Cover image: Edvard Munch, *The Kiss*. Image is in the public domain.

Contents

Ankle Socks

Richard liked her to wear ankle socks in the summer. He liked it when her legs became really brown and her feet white and innocent. It had been the tan lines on her feet from her sandals which had attracted him in the first place. But ankle socks were even better than sandals, though Viola didn't know quite why.

It had something to do with his childhood. There was a photograph of him on the wall of his study, near the window. A boyish version of him looking intently at a girl with bobbed brown her and wise, sad eyes. They both looked about nine, and there was something about the light that suggested an English summer. Viola came across him once, leaning against the wall, staring at the picture with a kind of hopeful, regretful look. He looked like a man shipwrecked, she thought. As if he had lost everything.

She never mentioned it. They didn't have that kind of relationship anyway, and neither of them wanted it. They wanted to love quietly, calmly, like adults, without the emotional storms that had wrecked both of them. They gave in to each other's fetishes and fascinations with good humour and without questions.

She didn't mind the ankle socks anyway. Not really. She would have drawn the line at anything with a frill of lace around the turnover. That really was childlike. They had no children and, having both been ruined as children themselves, didn't want any. It was funny how a pair of socks generated an entire outfit around themselves, and hair and makeup around that, and a persona around them in turn. The last time adult women could get away with ankle socks was the 1940s, she thought. Boxy shorts, floral blouses, and a scarf in their hair. A kind of fresh-faced Land Girl healthiness. Haystacks and Digging For Victory.

He came into the bedroom as she took her shirt off and crawled up the bed in her bra, shorts, and socks. She lay back and closed her

9

eyes. Richard sat at the foot of the bed and took her right foot in his lap. She opened one eye and watched his back, the shadows of the ivy dancing across the thin shirt she had bought for far too much in Grenada. She smiled at his shoulder, his ducked head holding her foot firmly. He turned it over, flexing the arch back and forward, cupping her heel, and pulled at her toes through the thin cotton.

Gently, he drew off the sock and wrapped the palm of his hand right around her foot, thumb to middle finger around the arch. She flexed her other knee and prodded him a little with the left foot. 'That can't smell nice.'

'Mmm, it's not bad. Loam and summer and sweat and you,'

'The poetry of foot odour. You could publish it. *The Odour Eaters*. Give Mark Haddon a run for his money.'

'No. Sun and summer and your sweet feet belong to me.'

She smiled again. The years of tacitly-agreed privacy, of knowing only the front rooms of each other, leaving everything else to stories which proved how different they were now – it all seemed worth it. Not that it had been hard. Living with someone, even – maybe especially, for ten years, who remained largely a mystery was what kept it going. Privacy made you continually new for each other. And honest with yourself about how lonely life really was, how it could only be faced with a calm heart and solitude.

She rubbed his back with her other foot. Silence, punctuated by the sound of the wood pigeons, lulled her. After a few moments she became aware that he was crying, silently, holding her pale foot, one hand cradling her toes with the chipped pink varnish on her nails. She sat up and touched his back.

'Richard?'

He stiffened. 'Richard. Why are you crying?'

He brushed the tears away roughly. 'Nothing. Sorry. Ignore it.'

'I can't ignore it. I've never seen you cry before. What's going on? It's not really my feet, is it?'

She watched his shoulders give a huge, convulsive shrug. 'You have such…It's stupid. You…they remind me of something. From a long time ago.' He shook his head.

She could see his eyes close briefly, as if he was in pain. She scooted forward and embraced him from behind, sliding her legs alongside his. 'Richard, I know we don't…we don't really talk about the past. Maybe less than most people. I'm fine with it, but …you can, you know, you can tell me anything.'

He said nothing for several long seconds. She brought her feet up, trapping him in the circle of her legs, her feet in his lap, one sock on and one off. He gripped her bare foot fiercely. 'You'd be horrified,' he said.

'Try me. And if I was, it doesn't matter, does it? Horrified or not, it's the fact of the past. And it's done.'

He looked out of the window at the ivy, waving like a handkerchief in a breeze that touched nothing else. She waited for his unwelcome story. She tried to assume the calm she remembered in her mother, whose talent for a kind of impassiveness brought out the worst of her teenage exploits.

'She … the little girl. In the picture. On the – '.

'I know. I know which one you mean.'

'She wanted to find this frog in the woods. It lived near pools, she said. She'd got this idea that some endangered species of frog was living in the stream that ran through the woods at the back of the house.'

'Who was she?'

'Her father was a sort of gamekeeper, odd-job man for the estate. Huge man. Drank and swore like a cauldron on fire. It was just the two of them. Her mother was dead. It had set him off.'

She thought about the child in the picture. 'She doesn't look like a happy child. In the photo, I mean.' She felt hot drops on her foot. The corner of his face showed a kind of furious concentration. 'But you were friends with her. That's good, Richard. It is.' She put her cheek to his back and felt it, wet with sweat and the tremours of withheld emotion.

'I loved her. I loved her. We were kids, but...you see it then, don't you? What people are really like. Straight as an arrow to the heart of her. I didn't even realize it. Like.... like living with a disease or something.'

'Not at all. Children love fiercely. They love truly and with complete, well, honour, I suppose. You're inside your own world and the little you know about yourself is completely known by the other. I suppose everything after that's a bit of a let-down.' She smiled ruefully.

'It wasn't like that, though. It was all wrecked. It was...' He gave a huge sigh, pushing her head off his back. She dropped her forehead back again.

'So did you find this frog?'

'We walked through the woods to the stream and she kept saying that she could hear it croaking. I couldn't hear it. I just became aware, as we walked, of how... I don't know, how *perfect* it all was. How perfect we were. It was all so clear, so sharp. Nothing, no sight, no place, no smell, no feeling of being in my own skin or being me with someone else, had ever been so perfect. The whole day felt as if it was, almost, I don't...shimmering.'

She nodded soundlessly against his wet shirt.

'We got to one of the pools near the river. It was just a kind of hole the size of a laundry basket full of muddy water. The stream flowed there sometimes and wore away the banks and made these sort of pot-holes.

'Anyway, we crouched down beside it and, my God, I can still smell the forest earth, and her hair, her smell. She didn't take a bath very often. They had no hot water and ...God, her pulse, I could see her heartbeat under her skin in her neck on the other side of her mud hole.'

He sank his head into his hands, his fingers in his hair. 'She put her arm in, right up to the elbow and felt around in the water, and I was getting ready to laugh at her and all of it even though I could have stayed there forever – I think part of me *has* stayed there for…as if I'm still there. Still there.

'She pulled her hand out and she actually had the thing! She really had got a frog.'

'One of the endangered ones?'

'God, I've got no idea. But she had this thing in her hand and it was blinking at her, at us, and, it was so *alive*, the whole moment was so alive. She had mud everywhere, on her shorts and her legs, her feet were covered in it. And I knew that she'd get a belting for it, but none of that seemed to matter. I mean, it was like … can you imagine *everything*, every idea about childhood being beautiful, and perfect, a perfect heart in a perfect place, completely outside of time?'

'I think so. I've never felt that, not when I was a child. But I know what you mean.'

'She was holding the thing up and laughing and I was laughing and then she opened her hand and the bloody thing jumped at me, and we laughed until we cried and then I … she looked … you had to see her face. It was like a candleflame, as though all of it was the flame and I was standing inside the flame. She was perfect. And I kissed her. I don't know; it just seemed the thing to do. You know, the way children do, sometimes?'

'I know.' She thought of greeting-card schmaltz. Cheap high street images of saccharin, adult-aped affection.

Another convulsive shudder. 'And the second I touched her lips I knew. It just hit me like, like a stench. Something rotten. She just immediately went kind of *soft*. As though she'd been kissed many, many times and she just automatically became unresisting. Sort of floppy and … my God, it was like, like putting rotten meat in your mouth when it had smelled so good. I just knew … that fucking man.'

He gave another shudder. She said carefully, 'But Richard, it wasn't her fault. I mean, these things spiral outwards, taint everything. You couldn't have done anything.'

'But the thing was, the moment, the perfect … it was all wrecked. It was *stained*. She was st—she could *never*, don't you see, see the perfect … she couldn't *know* how perfect …' He wheezed slightly. She heard a rattle under his ribs, as if the idea was pinballing around in his lungs.

'It was like seeing a snake. I, I … couldn't *not*. My God, I did it before I really understood what I'd done.'

Please don't have said that, she thought. Time felt like a kite string. She could just about reach the last inch of it with her fingertips if she stretched, to reel the last moment back in.

'My hand closed round a rock. A stone, really. A river rock. Flat thing.'

The breeze had dropped from around the ivy. 'I put her in a kind of … there was a hollow in the bank. Soft earth. One shoe came off. A sock. Last thing I saw … her little foot. In the earth of the bank. Dirt all got between her toes. Brown legs. Her feet. The stream running.'

Silence. A swallow. Her throat felt lumpy and tight. He hung his head like a marathoner. She wanted to yank her feet off his lap and shove them under the covers. Her feet, exposed. How could she walk barefoot up and down the rows of tomatoes in the garden again? How could she hide among the steeples of runner beans congratulating herself on this, the best of adulthood and childhood?

After a long moment she disengaged her feet from him, thankful she hadn't seen his face in it all. 'The afternoon's got away from me again,' she said, clambering off the bed. 'That's the last time I let you talk me into sleeping in the daytime.'

Atonement

A car clipped him as he left Habima Square at dusk. Just before his head struck the kerb he realized that they would strip him in the hospital. At the very least, take off his shirt. If he lost consciousness, he could not prevent them from doing it, and if they did that they would see. Then a great pain came down from the top of his head to his brow line, and he passed out.

He woke up in a curtained cubicle. His flute case was on the chair, along with his overcoat and suit jacket. He could see that the overcoat collar was lightly spattered with blood. He put a hand to his head and felt a tidy dressing over his right eyebrow and the familiar pull of stitches. Now his brow would be symmetrical, stitches on both sides.

Despite a wave of nausea and a headache that glowed, he felt for the bottom of his shirt and pulled it out of his belt. The bottom shirt buttons were still wrongly buttoned, which he had used for twenty-five years as his only way of knowing whether he had been undressed and redressed while unconscious.

The curtains parted with a tearing noise. A dark-haired nurse stood in the gap and looked at him. Automatically he calculated her age. A post-war baby. Maybe twenty-two now, so born just after. But she was dark, so maybe a sabra. Her name tag said *A. Kedar.* Was Kedar Hebrew? Lithuanian? Syrian? He still couldn't tell these things. Maybe Europe had no claims on her. So many maybes, but he still skipped a button at the bottom of his shirt, just to be sure.

How was he feeling, she asked. No dizziness, no nausea? He made a non-committal noise and touched the dressing. 'You?'

She nodded. She said he would be taken up to a ward for observation until they could discharge him into the care of a wife? A daughter?

No wife, no daughter, he said shortly. Israel was full of European men in their fifties who had no wife, no daughter.

He asked for his flute. She handed him the case, which had a heavy scuff on one corner. Someone had given it to the ambulance driver when they scooped him off Dizengoff Street. His name was on the card inside, but there was no telephone number. Just an address in Jaffa.

'You play with the philharmonic?'

He played with the philharmonic.

She put him in a wheelchair. He watched her put the cubicle back in order and admired her economy of movement, her calm precision. It was unwise to ask, but he liked to know that his guesses were still accurate. They had to be.

'You were a military nurse?'

She turned away as she answered. Until last week. In the Heights, where she had learned about concussions and stitching. She wheeled him up to the ward, chattering. He almost relaxed. She was *wahnsinnig*, a ditz. She brought him hospital-issue pyjamas. He said he would undress himself, and allowed himself a small twinkle at her. There was only, what, twenty? twenty-five? years between them. The awkwardness of attraction had always provided a good reason not to remove one's clothes around women.

He got into bed obediently. She hung his overcoat and suit on a hanger. 'I noticed the tattoo on your eyebrow,' she said.

He stilled, suddenly trapped beneath the white sheet and the Tel Aviv twilight floating through the window. 'The tattoo that is my eyebrow, you mean.'

'It's very good. Very well done. Was it done here?'

Was there a reason she had waited until he was on the second floor, in pyjamas, and in bed, before she asked this? He turned up his collar so that she would not see how fast his pulse drummed.

A German doctor, repairing a botched skin graft over a burn. He did not expect her to reply to this. Israel was full of European men in their fifties with scars they didn't want to talk about.

A horn blast made them both jump. The synagogue next door had installed a tannoy, she said, so that the patients could hear the shofar blown for Rosh Hashanah. He made another non-committal sound. Israel was full of European men in their fifties who had no time for High Holy Days.

A voice was coming over the tannoy, announcing first that it was testing, testing, then a sonorous wave of male song. She murmured that it was the day's parashah. She fiddled with the blind cord. He did not know whether pity moved him, or curiosity. He used to be sure of things like that.

'I'm not a religious man. Tell me what it says.'

'I call Heaven and Earth as witnesses today against you that I have set before you life and death, blessing and cursing, therefore choose life, that both you and your descendants may live...' she shook her head and let the blind cord go.

'You sound scornful.'

'My brother died in the Heights. I wonder if there is life, or endless war. Retribution that never stops. Trials that exhaust us. Justice that doesn't make us just.'

'What's left? You forgive those who try to wipe you out?'

She didn't know, she said. Maybe you stop when it's enough. You choose life, so you stop. Or you stop, and so you choose life. She didn't know.

She told him to rest, that breakfast would come at seven. That she had to go back to the emergency room. He lay down, reassured that the perilous moment had passed him by. Justice had brushed past him, but another war had taken the place of the last. Newer offences, newer griefs, newer vengeances, younger women with younger preoccupations, who chattered and could be charmed by older men. He checked his buttons out of habit and slept.

In the night she came. He felt her open his pyjama jacket and pull lightly on the skin of his bicep. He opened his eyes and saw her looking at the puckered cicatrix which covered the tiny tattoo.

17

Knowledge crossed her face, and decision, and he watched breathlessly through closed eyelashes as she rebuttoned the jacket and chose life for him.

An Old Bouquet

'A panini—a *panino*,' she corrected herself, 'with prosciutto and provolone. Do you want anything to drink?'

'Just one of the aranciatas.' He mangled it.

'*Ch*. It's aran-ch-yatta,' she said, smiling hard.

'Aranchyatta,' he said obediently. He caught her wrist as she turned to the door of the compartment. She stared at the filthy handle and the train corridor for a fraction of a second, then allowed him to pull her into a kiss.

She slid the door shut and turned in the direction of the trolley. It couldn't have moved beyond their carriage; he only went past a few minutes ago. She went past compartments with two or three people in each, strangers reading silently, checking phones, looking at the grim semi-industrial Italy that the guidebooks skipped over. Each person seemed wrapped in a civilized solitude, self-possessed and alone. She envied them.

Ahead, she saw the snack trolley. The panino would be about four Euros and the aranciata another three. Times two was fourteen Euros. She decided that she *would* have the panino and the drink and ignore the calories. Quickly, she reviewed her calorie intake of the previous two days and decided that she could do it, if they didn't then go out to another carb-and-fat loaded dinner when they arrived at Ravenna. Then being together in the hotel until bed. And then there was bed. A new city, a new hotel, the same pantomime and eventually moving onto the floor when he'd finished and she could be alone, even if it was on the carpet.

She shuffled along the swaying corridor, staggering and stopping every few feet. A tiny station, barely more than a platform and a name, shot past the window. What was life like in that place? What would her life be like if she got off there, vanished into the evening and tried to live, just live, from scratch, with nothing but what she had as she jumped onto the platform?

A crackle overhead and a stream of German, then Italian, announced that Barbiano was the next stop.

She sighed and moved along. They had sworn to try again. They had sat on the bed in Sydney, held hands, and sworn to draw a line under the past and make it all new from that moment on. As her lips promised, an inner voice prayed *create in me a clean heart, O my God. A clean heart.* Without resentment or remorse or regret, with a river of endless patience and no teeth-grinding at his ticks and lapses, the snoring and jerking, his clumsy love-making and eager, awkward conversation. A clean heart.

She flattened her back against a compartment door as the carriage rocked. The tendril of scent drifted up at the moment she was thrown off balance. Unbalanced, briefly vulnerable, then the scent of him—exactly as the sequence had been in the past, so it was then, right there, in a train corridor winding through northern Italy.

Her viscera reacted to the smell of him before her brain did. There, there among the filthy stale air, smudged thick with the smells of ancient cigarettes, heat, and seams of grime, was the scent of him, the man she had driven away, given up. Like a silver coin in the lining of a winter coat. She was transfixed, her back to the door of a compartment, her nose in the air like a hound, her eyes staring sightlessly into the corridor. The same gut-twisting leap was happening, the thought of him, the very possibility that he, who bore this mouth-watering, heart-wrenching smell, that he was close… She could not bear to move.

It was as though, in the clouds of steam which obscured her faith in life, a cool finger had touched the back of her sweating neck.

She pulled herself away from the compartment window. Time seemed to slow as she did so, and that old bouquet, a common scent worn by a million other men, but simmering with his exact warmth, his silken skin, showed her a vision of his head, dark and sleek as an otter's, bending over a book in the compartment.

He was not there. Of course he wasn't, she thought. Her heart slowed. She dropped her head to her chin, trying not to taste again that thin stratum of railway air that carried his perfume. Outside the corridor window the sun was dropping lower, vanishing behind houses, railway outbuildings, small Tyrolean churches. With each eclipse she saw her own face in the grimy glass, staring back at herself, lost, large-eyed, gaunt with disappointment and control.

Smears from the haze of dust obscured her face. The clean heart you pray for, it seemed to say, is as impossible as a clean face. There is no new start, no blank slate, only a long and filthy slog through the murk of desire and the sweat you work up by going through it.

A crackle repeated the approach of Barbiano. She hauled open the compartment door. Two middle-aged men in suits, typing on backpack-rested laptops, looked up. 'Excuse me,' she said. 'Do you speak English?'

One nodded. 'A little,' he said uncertainly.

The train began to slow as she explained the message. It came to a crisp halt at a short platform with a small, plain Tyrolean church beyond it. She turned the handle, stepped down on to the warm concrete and felt the bulk of the train begin to pull away as she slammed the door shut.

She had fourteen euros in her pocket. The Africans who peddled CDs outside the Prater probably made more than that in a day. Unburdened, with a clean heart, she began to walk slowly towards Barbiano.

Clothes Pegs

She wondered, *how long have we been hanging laundry out to dry?* Sarah had a sudden feeling that the unbroken chain of washings and dryings, heaving wet loads around and thinking about the weather - this was really the stuff of history. It went beyond the dates and places foisted on them at school, famous personalities and battles in Greek mountain passes. History was really about doing the washing.

Soon I won't be part of it any more, she thought. There was a lump in her breast that was gradually edging her out of the flow of time, like a fat person on a bus seat, gradually inching her out into the aisle. *I won't be here, but the Hills Hoist will be, and the washing will still need done. If it's not done Brian won't have clean clothes and that'll make him cross. If he's cross, customers won't ring him again when they need a plumber and he'll have no money. You can't survive on Centrelink so…*the tree of causes and effects got complicated at this point and branched off in different directions. She had never thought of herself as very clever and the chemo drugs made her head hurt when she thought hard, so it was easier to let it go.

She spun the hoist round one section and began with Sharon's t-shirts. The way the sections faced the sun pleased her. Brian's shirts and undies, Ben's rugby shirts and socks. There was something about doing the washing like this, where it all clicked into place, worked like a little machine. The tempo of her morning, the pace of the task, the sun and breeze, the number of items her family wore and how they fitted the lines strung within the hoist's spider web. It was efficient, beautiful, orderly.

As she reached up with the peg she felt a *snap-twang* in her collarbone area. It wasn't so much painful as surprising. 'Popping' was the cancer care nurse's term. She didn't much like the idea of things popping without her permission, but the whole breast cancer business had driven home the fact that she had very little control over anything.

Which was why she was particularly happy with the laundry. That much, she could do.

She still hadn't worked out how she really felt about dying. She'd cried, once she was safely outside the clinic, but she wondered privately if it hadn't been from relief at getting away from the oncologist's diploma-filled room.

Brian had been knocked silly by it, but he seemed to be over the drinking and crying. They'd even had a brief argument the previous night. The whole business of dying could have been a dream.

She dug around in the peg bag. She would need to buy a new bag and more pegs, if Brian and Ben were going to do the washing between them. Brian wouldn't understand her attachment to the old mildew-spotted peg bag that had been her mother's and since Ben lost everything, he would definitely lose clothes pegs. Briefly, she feared for the washing machine and made a mental note to leave the warranty somewhere obvious.

She had walked, what? Hundreds - no, maybe even thousands - of kilometres around this Hills Hoist, pegging out washing, following the wind and the sun. If she laid all those kilometres in a straight line, where would they take her? She didn't want to be anywhere else. Home was as close and as far away as she had ever been. A deeply-grooved circle in the back yard, as deep as a thousand kilometres would have been.

She ran a testing hand down one of Ben's socks. The heat had taken the moisture clean out of it in the time she had taken to fill the last section of the line. This was the heat of the suburbs furthest west of the city. No sea breeze, no river, just a five-thousand-kilometre stretch of nothingness until the ocean on the continent's western seaboard. The suburb where the poor migrants from Sudan came, where the poorest whites could afford to build.

I'm poor, I'm youngish, I'm dying, she thought. She clutched at Ben's socks, thinking of how she wouldn't live to see any grandchildren's feet grow to match her son's. *Why don't I mind more? Why am I not desperate, bargaining, grieving for myself?*

She reached up to take the pegs off the line. Pinching the ends together, one peg collapsed in dry pieces, fragments of plastic, a spring, the other side still whole. She looked at the remains of the peg. She had bought them in a pack of a hundred from the two-dollar store only last year. They had been clipped, row on grey plastic row, to a strip of cardboard. Like girls, she remembered thinking, in their school uniforms ready to be unpegged and sorted out among homes. Now one little year had done for it. The sun had beaten out whatever it was that held it together, bleached its gloss off, shuffled apart the onionskin layers until, unable to perform its one simple action, it shattered.

She held the fragments of peg in her hand for a little while and closed her eyes as her family's washing spun around her in a gentle breeze. A shirt sleeve, clean and fresh, a singlet, a towel, and in and out flashed the sun, the beating sun.

Binocular

The branch pulled at his jumper. It was surprisingly uncomfortable lying along it. He had everything: snacks, a water bottle, the new lanyard on his binoculars, a warm beanie and gloves with the tactile rubber dots on the fingers so that he could manipulate the lenses. It looked OK when he put it all in his backpack. Just another kid going somewhere in the autumn twilight.

Anyway, it wasn't as if he was going to be there all night. He could surely put up with the hard bulk of the branch against his chest as he lay along it, at least for a few hours. There was no other spot so perfect. Just behind the tumbledown, creosote-roofed shed in the bottom corner of the garden. The tree faded into the jumbly background of allotments and ramshackle shed-life where her garden ended. He could climb it with relative ease. This was important, because he'd always been a poor climber. A poor specimen generally, which was made abundantly clear to him at least once in a school day. He could stand on a sagging pile of forgotten potting mix bags and hoist himself up, then up again to the first big branch, and drag himself along it, camouflaged in its tunnel of leaves. He would lie there like a caterpillar, cocooned in army surplus and expectation, as evening fell and she came home for the night.

She left the shop punctually at 5.30, when the rush of people buying frozen dinner, frozen desserts, and sweet, cheap fizzy drinks was over. It took her fifteen minutes to walk from the end of the shopping precinct to the first battered row of houses on the estate. From there it could be anything between five and twenty minutes to her door, depending on whom she ran into.

He lay along the branch, knee to throat going numb under the pressure, and imagined her in the shop pulling off her pinafore, slipping a purple-nailed hand through the peeling gold chain of her handbag, and calling goodbye to the other women. Then footfalls on the darkening pavement, past mesh grilles on the windows of the bookmakers, the bottle shop, the electronics repair place that was always mysteriously closed. At Singh's kids' clothes shop she often paused for a fraction and looked at the poly-nylon confections with spangled skirts and puffed sleeves for Pakistani princesses. She always seemed to set her face a little harder after Singh's and walk more deliberately, as if the sight of the kids' clothes had reminded her of something she'd missed out on, but which couldn't be helped now.

He didn't know why she had no kids. It was what women did. They had a couple, and then you got moved into a house of your own, and you scraped by for a bit until the kids were older, then they did the same. They were just more names to remember when you met them on the estate, pushing the littlest one around in a buggy, trying to make it play among the weeds and broken bottles near the swings. Even the names were limited; weird spellings of whoever was on the England team, for boys, or their Brazilian girlfriends, for girls.

He was thinking about this when her light snapped on, illuminating the rectangle of her bedroom. She always left the downstairs lights off and stomped up the stairs to the bedroom. He thought it must be lonely for her. She was only seventeen, which wasn't that old, even on the estate, and her father appeared only intermittently. It made her seem like a princess in a tower, he thought. Lots of long blonde hair and only darkness below her lighted turret.

He checked his watch. His hands tightened around the binoculars. He hadn't watched her for weeks. She'd gone away somewhere for a month and he was trying to break himself out of the habit of watching anyway, which he felt somehow wasn't helping him. Tonight though, she didn't start peeling off the layers of discount-rail polyester underneath the hot pink parka. She stood at the window, her head tilted a little into the lace curtain, and stared out at the allotments, the autumn smoke and extravagant, tragic twilight. She looked tired and sad, and this reassured him that she hadn't discovered him, but was looking beyond his perch to the season and the gentle decaying mulch of the world.

It was his undoing, because he was so intent on the meaning of her stare that he overbalanced and rolled off the branch, plunging to the compost bags below with a strangled cry. He struck the rotting plastic with a solid, damp sound and lay staring up at the bare branches as his wind returned. The binoculars' lanyard had caught on a stubby branch and dangled there, unharmed. He closed his eyes in shame.

A door slammed open, then slammed shut, and there was the sound of running feet, and he knew she'd discovered him, plummeting earthwards. There was no point trying to leg it. He couldn't leave the binoculars and he wasn't quick enough to get a head start.

Her trainers hoved into view, squashing the beech leaf carpet. Profanities rained down on him. 'What the fuck d'you think you're doing?' He was afraid she'd kick him. He rolled into a ball, squishing himself against the bark. 'Were you spying on me, you fuckin' little perv?'

He shook his head, rubbing his nose against his kneecaps. She reached over him and yanked, ineffectually, at the dangling binoculars. 'You was up that tree with them binoculars, fuckin' waitin' for me to get my kit off,' she said wonderingly.

He stared miserably into the darkness of his protective curl. Suddenly she laughed, a shrill, unpleasant laugh. He pulled his head up. 'I didn't mean nothin'. I wasn't gunna take pictures or anything. I'm really sorry. Please, just…can I go – I won't do it again, I just…I'm sorry.' He ground to a halt. She wasn't listening. Her face, upturned to the streaky sky, was still creased in a rictus of laughter. His heart misgave in his chest.

He struggled to his feet. She was still laughing. If he returned without the binoculars, Bill'd leather him, but it was better than listening to her hysterical giggle in the autumn air. He turned, but she caught his arm in a pincer-sharp grip. 'No you don't. You wanted to see me – well, fuckin' come an' see me.' She turned back to the house, dragging him with her. He struggled, the way small children squirm and struggle in shopping trolleys, without much hope of release. She had only to ring the cops and he'd get done as a sneaking juvenile perv. A fat one at that, he thought.

She dragged him to the garden, in the back door, and through the kitchen, then pushed him in front of her up the stairs like a recalcitrant dog, jabbing his back. At the top of the stairs she spun him through a door and tossed him onto a bed like a shopping bag. He folded himself like a winkle against the wall.

She stood against a chipped particle-board dresser, breathing hard. 'Wha's yer name?'

'Kevin.'

She snorted. Her bed was squashy and covered in a set of pink and purple covers. His mum had the same set, bought on sale from Argos.

He said foolishly. 'My binoculars. They're not mine. They're me stepdad's. He'll do me if I lose 'em.'

She stared out the window at the last streaks of purple. 'Shurrup,' she said softly.

Cautiously, he withdrew his head from his knees. She stared back at him, thoughtful and terrible at the same time. 'What did you think you'd see?'

He shrugged unhappily. 'Dunno.'

'Like lookin' at girls, do ya?' She didn't sound angry. He shrugged again.

'Think we're all soft and pretty with nice hair? All long and girly, like?'

He was confused. 'Dunno. I s'pose.'

She fingered her blonde fringe. It hung dead straight over her forehead. She inserted a finger underneath and in a single swift

28

movement, pulled off her hair. A bald scalp, white and fragile as a battery hen's egg, shone in the weak bedroom light.

His mouth dropped open. She looked ageless, sexless, unformed as a doll, like a human template, before individualising. 'Weren't expecting that, were ya?'

She slipped both arms out of the hoodie that said *No Doze* across the chest. It crumpled around her waist and then dropped to the floor, unimpeded by hips. She discarded the shapeless outsize t-shirt beneath it. A singlet like a child's was underneath, some delicate, much-washed lace curling over the neckline. It sagged against her thin torso, competing with her ribs and clavicle for grey shabbiness.

She lifted her arms over her head and pulled off the child's vest. He gave a strangled sound of shock, disgust, perhaps even admiration.

She pointed to the diagonal keloid scars where breasts had been. 'Cat gotcha tongue? I thought boys liked scars. You ain't gonna find ones like this, anyway. Not round here.'

He heard his own heart beating, incongruous in the twist of purple-pink bedclothes. There was a low crackling of static, which he realised was time, passing. Her shoulders sagged a little. 'At least you ain't run away.'

He swallowed. 'What …what 'appened?'

'Breast cancer. What did you think, moron?' She shrugged. 'Not that they was worth shoutin' about before, but. You can get a reconstruction – have a fake pair put in. That's two years on a waitin' list. Or buy a bra with a fake pair sewn in.' She sniggered. 'Like TV dinner. Ready Tits.'

He laughed, then bit his lip. She flared up. 'That's what they all do. Laugh and then stop like it's a sin or I'm some sort of fuckin' terminal case. Like I'm gunna die or bite em.' She laughed a broken sound. 'That's the best bit. Can't even do that.' She put a hand to her mouth and withdrew a top and bottom denture, spittle-dripping and shiny.

He stared at the caved-in mouth, the vanished lips. He remembered Halloween crones, toothless and wizened, hanging by their hats in the corner shop. 'Fing is, ev'ryone finks is mefmaf,' she said. He was shocked to hear her speak. *It shouldn't be talking*, he thought. 'Can you put em back in?' he said in a tiny voice. ' 'S hard to…'

She put the dentures back in with a swallowing motion. He caught his face twisting in disgust and rubbed his nose to hide it. 'What d'you say?'

'Meth-mouth,' she said. 'If I leave 'em out, everyone thinks I done meth.'

It occurred to him that she might actually be dying. He might be talking to a dying person.

'So …is it like, fatal?'

She pulled out the chair and sat down. She looked at him in the mirror, a heap of boy on the Turkish Delight bed. 'Nuh. This is it. What's left. I gotta have checks every six months. But the surgeon said there weren't anything left for the cancer to take hold of.' She looked at herself, as if there were nothing remotely discoverable any more in the mirror's reflection. 'Just left me lookin' like a frickin' alien and moved on.'

He scooted to the edge of the bed. She saw him. 'Go on, then, piss off. You've had your fright. Go and tell your friends you got a striptease from a girl with no tits and no hair. And no teeth. You'll be an effin laughin' stock.'

'I wasn't gunna,' he said indignantly. 'I was just gonna say you could get a tat on your…" he waved a finger vaguely in the direction of his chest. 'Cover up them scars. You could get a really big one, like…like…'

'The Arsenal crest?' she said scathingly. '*I LUV WENGER?*'

'No, like, flowers," he said. ' 'Cos you already got the lines.' He drew diagonals on his own jumper. 'It's like a snowdrop, and the dots,' he shuffled off the bed and came tentatively towards her, pointing at the pin-prick suture marks on either side of the scar, '…they're like the flowers. Or you could do bluebells. Or wheat.' He stood back and looked critically at her mutilated chest. 'Or a big poppy, like, all soft and silky petals.' He saw himself in the mirror, discovering the possibilities of a garden on her wrecked skin. He blushed and turned away.

There was an awkward silence. When he looked up she was examining her chest, turning this way and that in the poor light. 'Yeah, maybe,' she said.

She sighed and slumped, her thin shoulder blades standing out like pyramids on her back. He had the feeling that he was watching time eat someone alive. A private operation which usually happens unseen, unconsciously. She tied a blue scarf around her skull and faced him. ' S'pose you wanna go home now?'

He wriggled awkwardly. 'It's late. My mum'll be at me if I miss tea. It's my stepdad's night at the club. She doesn't like being alone in the evening.'

'I know how she feels,' she said, pulling her shirt over her head. The scars vanished.

'You could come home with me,' he said shyly. 'My mum'd like you."

She examined him closely. 'What, the baldy freak? Nah. Thanks though. I've got the telly and my phone. An' I got work tomorrow, anyway.'

He stared into the corner. 'Maybe come another time.'

She smiled, a little smile. 'Yeah, maybe.' She clasped her hands between her knees. 'Well go on, Kevin the Perv. You learned your lesson. Don't climb up no more trees to spy on girls. You never know what you'll find.'

His hand was on the door handle. 'Can I come back, some time. Just, like, to chat?'

She snorted. 'Yeah, all right. Leave them binoculars at home.' She turned back to the mirror. He clattered down the stairs in a rustle of anorak and backpack.

In the kitchen a sad little dinner was defrosting on the counter, the cardboard box sodden and sagging. A wizened Granny Smith sat in the fruit bowl, its sweet reek hanging in the air. Next time, he thought, he would bring apples, the best of the late autumn. He would put red apples in the fruit bowl, draw her out of the turret and away from the mirror, and discover whatever was left of the year, with her.

Hair

The most profound actions are unaccompanied by words. The same action is repeated again and again throughout time.

She finds his ward, closes the door, and draws the curtain across the small window.

He is asleep, inside a protective tent which shields him from airborne disease. His body, ravaged by the microbes picked up from a stream in the Panjshir Valley, is a shadow of the man who looked like a god, rowing stroke in the University boat.

It is a year since the quarrel and she stands, looking through the plastic at his sleeping face, feeling at once grateful and terrified.

She puts the jar on the bedside locker and takes off her jacket. She locks the door and removes her shoes, stockings, and sweater. There is no movement in the hot, hospital-grade air, boiled clean and stinking of worry and last breaths.

She stands at the foot of his bed and loosens the plastic, then the heavy white knitted cotton blanket. He sleeps on, unaware of her and of the year that has passed.

His feet and thin ankles appear, white as the threadbare, boiled linen, flexed and askew with the ease of sleep. She sweeps her long plait over her shoulder and takes out the elastic, unfurling her hair into three kinked, silken snakes, twining sinuously down her left breast, pooling on the sheet.

And then she takes his feet in her hands and allows the tears to fall. A stream of tears, a flow as of rain from a tree's branches to the soil. She holds his feet and adores him, weeping for the quarrel and for lost time and for him, so nearly lost, so nearly found.

Her grief abases her before God, and she begs for another chance – no, not even for so much, but simply to remain at his feet and for the blood to remain flowing through them and their hearts to remain beating. It is enough.

33

In the deep valley of sleep, where he can smell the snows of Panjshir and the stillness of stones in these dry valleys, he feels rain on his feet. Warm, living silk, caressing the aching tops of his feet, brushing his toes, curling around his ankles like a cat.

Up he moves, up to the light, which is still and dry as the valleys of Herat, still and tasting of death and of lands hostile to men. He opens his eyes and sees at his feet the woman, weeping to wash them, taking her hair in hand to dry them.

He sees her take the jar from beside the bed – it is all as silent as the valleys have been in his head, for a year or longer – and break it open. She pours a little oil onto her cupped hand and brings it to his foot. It slides onto his thin skin, a tiny friction brushing the hairs backwards.

A scent is released within the plastic tent. It smells of spice and heat, adoration and wealth, of opulent, elegant gifts. It smells of her heartbreak and the reverence twined into her hair, which binds her to him on his sickbed.

She bends to his feet and kisses them, wiping tears from her cheeks with the same handkerchief of hair. Her glossy crown, enslaved by her sorrow and her gratitude for his life.

Up the bed her eyes travel, and they light on that well-loved face, now a map of ridges and caves of suffering. He has gone where even God has forgotten, and he has come back to her.

On this Kiss

She smelled of leaf mulch and cold. It wasn't a body smell at all, which made Simon relieved. He'd been expecting the smell of decay – he'd caught a whiff of bad meat once, walking past a butcher's shop, and imagined it was something like that.

This makes it sound as though he'd thought about it for a long time, which isn't quite true. He'd seen the girl a few minutes previously, when he came into the clearing and found her body lying under the bare trees, the last leaves of autumn drifting down into her hair.

Simon would have been ashamed if anyone had seen his lack of concern. He'd parked concern about other people's opinions, though, back on the road with his car. He felt as he always felt when he was alone in the woods, absolutely sure of a few things, the only things that concerned him. He supposed it was what Thoreau had meant by living deliberately. Somehow, it meant that finding a random corpse in the woods didn't feel surprising.

He approached her unhurriedly. He didn't look around to see if he was alone. Only people with a guilty conscience do that and – although it might seem creepy, and although random men alone in the woods approaching stone-cold girls under trees might seem guilty of something to *us* – Simon certainly didn't feel guilty of anything.

He wasn't a rapist, a stalker, a survivalist, or even a naturist. He just liked being alone in the quiet woods with his dog, who was off somewhere scaring things in the undergrowth. He saw a girl under a tree. He knew what girls were, and trees. He knew that people die. Put those three known things together and it's perfectly rational not to fuss when you come across a dead girl under a tree. The forthcoming kiss, I grant you, doesn't fit with all of that, but you cannot tell children fairy tales and not expect them to produce unusual results.

But as he walked across the clearing, feeling the thick carpet of leaves bounce and sigh under his weigh, with autumn all around him, he was more than just Simon-who-has-a-dog-and-a-duplex. He was a man alone in the woods, where men are princes or huntsmen, royal messengers, or outlaws subject only to the laws of the seasons. Women, by the same logic, are princesses, little girls lost, or witches.

So there he stands, looking down at her, wondering how long she's been there. He knows, with the same certainty that he knows evening will fall, that he'll kiss her. Secretly, he also feels slightly squeamish at the thought that maggots may be fattening themselves on her decaying sweetness. So he smells her first, cautiously, like a dog.

He notices how fine her red-gold hair is, strewn among the leaves. He remembers a poem he read about a knight 'with red-gold glamour, a knight in the wheat', and it seems to make sense now. He brushes a finger over the collar of her woollen sweater, which is dark blue, and made of very fine wool. Her legs are bent slightly, like a sleeper's, and her brown leather hiking boots are new. He sniffs again, but all he smells is cold and the great forests of the Pacific northwest.

She looks like many young women with red gold hair. Fine-boned, a light scatter of auburn freckles across her face, an elegant mouth with unchapped lips and the finest tracery of lines beginning to show around it. It's impossible to get a sense of someone when they're asleep.

He cocks his head this way and that, trying to work out what the best angle of approach is. There are a few rocks scattered on the other side of her, which would be in the way if he moved to the other, more convenient, side. He leans right over and steadies himself with a hand on either side of her head.

And kisses her.

A man in the woods kissing a dead girl that he's found lying beneath a tree. It's not intended to be the kiss of life, but it might as well be. Underneath the soft pressure of his lips, she draws a great breath, like a sigh, and opens her eyes.

'What are you doing?'

He rocks back on his heels and stares at her for a second, feeling the shockwave of their mutually-exclusive fairy tales clash and eddy. From his perspective, this bit *is* unexpected. And disquieting. He feels like a scab being pulled away from a wound. The scab is Simon-with-a-dog-and-duplex, and the wound is Simon-alone-in-the-woods. This explains why he takes one of the rocks and beats her over the head with it.

He doesn't see whether she's dead (again) or not. He whistles for the dog, walks back up to the road with the rock in his hand, and shuts the car door as a sense of evening seeps coldly into the air.

Are you disappointed? What sort of denouement can there be for this brief event? Don't forget – keen readers heartily endorse this whole kissing-in-the woods business. Without that drive which makes a young man, alone in the woods, kiss some beautiful but entirely random dead girl, we would have no fairy tales. Whether he marries her or murders her is immaterial. That comes after the kiss, for which we cannot chastise him without getting rid of men altogether. Events, which are individual, are not the same as drives, which are universal. It's hardly a horror story, this. On this kiss in the woods is built all our happily ever afters.

Tub

We ate early. I stacked the dishes in the sink and wandered into the garden. The weeds were so high I couldn't tell where the boundary with the field was. Hayseed clung to me, spitting seeds into my dress. I'd have to have a shower again or I'd itch all night.

An ancient crab apple tree grew in front of a rough stone wall. A half-tumbled arch had once marked passage between orchard and what? Potager? Flower garden? Having met her once in my extreme youth, I couldn't imagine what Aunt Nelly (I was already beginning to think of her as a real aunt, as communal property, which would have made me his cousin, or maybe not-quite-sibling) would have planted.

I felt the grass part before him. I felt the evening sun on my face and his warmth at my back. He stretched an arm to the lintel stone on the arch, jagged and protruding. 'Careful of this'.

We passed into the enclosed space. Any planting design had long ago been taken over by meadow grass, poppies, stray wheat. A wild garden – order corrupted, but delightfully. In the shade of the wall I spied something with regular lines.

A bathtub, once upon a time enamelled whitely, now full of black water and mud, green grass growing through the overflow vent. Its was battered along one side, cowslips masking the black patches. He grimaced. 'I'd forgotten about that.' He looked at me. 'Do you remember?'

I didn't remember.

He sat carefully on one lip, and pulled me down to sit in the grass before him. 'I washed you in this bath when you were, what, four? Five? Tiny.' His fingers ticked against the fawn duck, stretched tight over his thigh. 'Nelly came in. She saw…I don't know. I don't think I know what she saw. She can't have seen anything, I think. But she felt something. You don't remember?'

I made a movement with my eyebrows. The world was rose-gold and we had our own wilderness and Nelly wasn't there. He took my hands. 'You were sent straight to bed, I remember that. She stayed up there with you for – God, it seemed like hours. Asking questions. Prodding. I was packed off home the next morning. I didn't see her again.' He looked at his hands. 'Nor you, not for years.'

I had a dark, dim memory of the bedroom in the attic and Nelly's angular, disapproving weight squashing the comforter. Questions and wishing she would leave me in the wonderful dark with the lime tree shadows. 'So what had she seen? Or not seen? What did you do?'

He threw up his hands. The sudden movement rocked the bathwater which plashed a muddy backslap on his thigh. 'Nothing! I didn't lay a finger of desire on you until what – fifteen? Sixteen? Years later.'

'But you looked.' I thought about it. 'Even then? So small? So samey? Aren't kids all the same?'

He looked towards the wheatfield. The low sun struck his jaw and put a slash of gold down the side of his face like a scar. 'It wasn't like that. I just remember looking at you in the water, so little and … unformed, I suppose, and thinking how attached to me you were, and how you would change, all that baby softness would turn into straight lines, and the world would plane you down and make you sharp and … and I suppose I thought, would you love me then? When there's so much more world, so many more things between us? And how I wanted you like that, grown up, but like a kid too, all clear and peaceful and knowing what you thought about me, and you … without fools like Nelly and all that …' he waved in the direction of the house. 'All that, wrecking it.' He sighed.

His head hung, the sun striking the crown, shining brighter than the silver threads. I put a hand on the inside of his knee. 'So what about the bathtub?'

'Nelly ripped it out. Redid all the bathrooms. Locks on all the doors. Turned the room I'd slept in into some sort of box room. She never had Michael or me again. Elizabeth, though. But not me, ever. My mother couldn't understand it. She thought I must have been rude to the vicar or something.'

'I never knew,' I said, thinking. There I'd been – there we'd been, already rumbled ten years before anyone had cause. And I'd been oblivious. The first of several crosses he'd carried for me, I suppose. 'We can put it back. Clean it out, if you like. Re-do the enamel.'

He shook his head. 'I can't even remember which bathroom it was. You can't scrub out the past, anyway.' He stood, carefully. The water slopped and tilted in the scratched tub. I put a hand on the enamel, trying to remember a boy's hope for love in the future as he looked at a child. The cruel, caustic suspicion of a widow watching from the doorway. No, the memory was as overgrown as the garden.

I led him back to the house and thought about how love, like a garden, runs riot and grows wild and peaceful without the restraining hand of some damn gardener and all their plans.

Daisy Chain

The place smelled of hair product, synthetic strawberry, and sex. Under those smells was the building's old smell of dust, disuse, and old metal.

Alice put her case on an old machine table, to which someone had attached handcuffs, one pair at each side. The table was stamped *Hughes & Sons – Sheffield, England.*

The director – Alice assumed he was the director, anyway – was pacing in a corner beside an incongruous Chinese screen. Behind the screen, by the warehouse windows, was a king-size bed on which two naked girls were lying, playing with their phones. At the foot of the bed a naked man was playing with his phone, one knee drawn up under his chin. A second man was sitting cross-legged on the floor atop a North Face parka, also with his phone. Also naked. A large camera on a dolly with a short run of track curving around the bed, seemed to be supervising them, a set of headphones perched on top.

She got out her kit and went to the bed, nodding at the director as she passed. He gave her a thumbs up and pointed to one of the girls before turning away again and explaining to someone that the warehouse had been lent by a friend on the proviso that a part be written in for him.

There was a blonde and a brunette. They both had enhanced breasts which sat atop their rib cages pointing straight up despite their flat position. She was reminded of shield bosses in museums. The blonde turned over, her eyes locked to her phone. Her buttocks had obviously been enhanced too. There was a tiny silvery scar beneath the oaken tan where something had obtruded – air? silicon? fat? – into her glutes.

'I'm Alice,' she said, pulling her gloves on. They were unnecessary, since there would be no gun, no needles. But she wanted to do it quickly and cleanly and get to her life drawing class in the evening. 'Who am I doing?'

The brunette gave her a smile. 'Me, please,' she said, peaceably. 'But nothing permanent. My mum'd have a fit if I went home with tatts.'

The other girl and the guy at the end of the bed laughed. Alice got out the ditto paper, primer, sponges and a can of fixative spray. She leaned over the girl, who smelled of watermelon and exercise. The light was excellent, clear and pale, a completely unsympathetic, truthful light. The girl's skin was beautiful. Fine-grained, almost flawless except for some stretch marks around her nipples and over Cooper's ligaments where the breast attached to the body.

'I'm going to put a tribal band here,' Alice said, running a latex finger along the girl's chest in a line beneath her breasts. 'And maybe something going from your navel around your hip, though that might smudge.'

'I can stay off it,' the guy said, seriously. 'I'll just hold her somewhere else.' He looked like an apprentice tradesman, she thought, talking about the girl as if she was a problem plumbing job. He patted the girl's foot. 'Plenty of other places.' The girl gave him a fond poke with her toe.

The four actors talked quietly while Alice did the tribal band, then a drift of frangipani around the girl's hip, and a small chain of daisies around her slender ankle. It was all just flash from the shop, but she had drawn the daisy chain herself and was thinking about putting it on her own ankle. It felt strange to touch a body which maintained itself by being only that – a body, doing body things with other bodies, for the edification of brains they would never meet. She told herself this was a stupid distinction; there was no difference between the fawn-slender leg of this brunette who made a living having sex before a camera, and the well-tanned limbs of the wealthy housewives who did the same thing without the camera.

Maybe, she thought, it was the knowledge of it – the bodiness of what that body was doing, and why. She held the girl's ankle up while the fixative spray dried. Could you feel honesty in flesh? The girl's body was a conscious canvas upon which desire was projected. It was the consciousness that made the difference. Or maybe it was just a cheaper tan than the North Shore housewives.

There was a sudden noise like clapping, as a pair of pigeons departed a ledge from the windows above them. A single small feather and a shower of down and dust-motes drifted around in a finger of sunlight. The four actors looked up into the clear light. Alice was aware of a strangely beautiful moment: the drifting feather, the glassy clarity, the naked people on the bed turned serpentinata to the source of the noise. It was like an afternoon on Mount Olympus, she thought, these somehow super-real people, lazing around between bouts of passion as real as they were stylized, the slow good humour of them, the slender relationship to real life. Beside them she felt like an armature, a pencil sketch.

She got up from the bed. The director was off the phone and looking expectantly at them. 'I'm done,' she said. 'Just try not to grab her where I've placed them. The spray's good against sweat and water, but not deliberate smearing.'

'Dan's a pro,' said the director, inspecting the girl's chest and hip. 'What's on your leg?'

The girl obediently lifted her leg in a seamless moment to his eye, exposing a sex so hairless it looked unfinished. 'A daisy chain?' said the director. 'Is that a joke?'

Alice realized the rebus, and blushed. 'Actually,' he said, 'we could add that in, just before the money shot. The first one, I mean. That's a good idea – we could have Carmen and Dan against the, that table thing, and Nikko and Candice on the other side and ... if we could fit one more girl in...'

He turned to ask Alice if she'd care to join, but she had already gone.

Dionysus

She paid for him online. She didn't like the idea of having so much cash around; she might be paying but biology still obtained, making him stronger than her. Or she hoped so. She'd send him back if he wasn't.

He was very little like the image on the agency site but she was used to that. In real life there were shadows around his eyes that had clearly been photoshopped out of the profile picture. She was surprised by this. It gave him dimension, which anyone selling men to women would have known was attractive, and therefore expensive. It made him seem, not *older*, she thought, but ageless. Beyond age, anyway.

She shut the door after him and led him to the sitting area, which smelled of vacuum cleaning and hotel furniture polish. She leaned back in the overstuffed armchair and looked at him while he, professionally, sat still and allowed himself to be looked at. Looked over. There was a tiny smile, a seed-leaf of a smile, somewhere around the corners of his mouth and this annoyed her.

'What's your name?' She reached for the bottle of white wine beside the chair. She wondered whether to pour any for him. She was still annoyed at the smile but being ungenerous would mean her annoyance had mastered her.

'Edmond.'

'Really?'

'Really.'

She didn't particularly care whether it was his real name or not. She asked because it allowed her to gauge how good he was at lying. She was paying to be set free from something that prevented her from giving her full concentration to whatever she chose. She poured two glasses and took a sip of her own before putting his before him. Like a baby, she thought. That made her feel better.

'So Edmond. What are you particularly good at?'

This bit always bored her. They rattled off a list of things as though going through aisles in a hardware store. They were usually proficient, and if they weren't, they could usually supply chemicals that allowed her to believe they were. She didn't particularly care how hard they worked for her orgasm; it wasn't genuine, and it wasn't permanent. She accepted the limits of things.

Edmond sipped his wine. 'I'm good at bargaining.'

She didn't know what to make of that. It exposed to her how often she had played this carpet-seller-and-tourist game, and how she wrong-footed herself each time by falling into light verbal sparring.

'I'm not.'

He took another sip. 'I know.'

She stood up. He stood up too; she saw that he knew the trick of standing when she did, to make his greater height and bulk subtly apparent. Overshadowing but not overpowering.

She drew him to the bed and slid his jacket from his shoulders. She was glad when he didn't prissily pick it up and smooth it, showing how much more he loved his tailor than making five hundred an hour for the pleasure of fucking a surgeon who smelled of French perfume and Turkish coffee.

He untied his tie and let her loosen the top two buttons of his shirt. Something occurred to her and she stopped halfway through the third button. 'Have you had to bargain often?' She thought for a second, wondering what she was asking. 'Not like this, I mean...' She realized she wasn't sure what she meant, but she recognized that five hundred didn't cover whatever it was.

'Not often. But once it was for everything I wanted.' He was looking at her, but she watched his throat as he spoke.

'Was it worth it?' For some reason, it seemed pointless to ask what he had wanted, and where, and why.

'No.'

She continued undoing the buttons, then pushed the shirt open, still tucked into his belt. He didn't have the usual carefully gym-fit, machine-tanned, waxed and polished pristineness which always made her roll her eyes internally. There was an old tan-line where a t-shirt had begun and ended, and beneath it he was pale, with a kind of sinewy leanness that reminded her of a whippet. Something thin and single-minded.

There was a thick, ragged scar on the right side of his chest. Left-handed assailant, she thought immediately. Unusual. Silently she mapped his inside. Upper apex of the right lung, just missing hemothorax and lung collapse. Lucky boy. He didn't look like a fighter, and the callouses on his hands, the still-evident tiny tan line around his second knuckle, said he had used an assault rifle and fingerless gloves somewhere hot, where a bare, bright sun shone on his hands.

He wore a thin leather cord around his neck. She fingered it, and a heavy coin slipped around and landed in the Plender gap. He obviously slid it around to the back when he was working. Didn't women like the bling - or did he think she'd steal it?

A chunky thing, for a man so slight, so practical. It was unpolished and rough around the edges. She looked more closely. A naked man, stepping forward in dance, carrying a flaming torch in each hand, carelessly, and a lionskin draped around his arms like a film star's stole.

She ran her finger along the tan line, and down to the scar. 'Does it go with these?'

'It does.'

'Dionysus,' she said. 'The twice-born, the god who comes. The liberator, the foreigner.' She remembered several other things about Dionysus, but these involved gangs of women going mad, and mothers eating the hearts of their unborn children.

'Dismembered and put back together.'

46

She picked it up from his collarbones. Not one of these men had ever told her the truth about anything, but she didn't mind being lied to for five hundred an hour. What she minded was how limited their lies were. She despised lies that were designed to appease. There was no point in asking about the coin. He would either refuse to explain it or tell her a lie which showed what strangers they were to each other.

He saw her looking, and she saw that he saw. There was a long moment where their mutual observation wandered into the silent space of antagonism. The friction between a woman who pays to be fucked and a man who lives by fucking. Then it wandered out again and the antagonism was gone, only a man and a woman and a coin from far away and long ago.

'Is this what you bargained for?'

He closed a hand over hers. The coin bit slightly into her palm. 'I was paid once, to do something I didn't want to do.'

'And you keep the coin why?'

'To remind me that once, I could be bought.'

She decided to take that as a compliment. Later, he didn't sleep, though she fell into a light doze, and dreamed of a scorching sun across her skin like sandpaper, and a lion's head swinging between a man's thighs, and flames. Somewhere in the distance there was the sound of a woman weeping, and a gunshot.

The Swimmer

Later, I told myself that I hadn't consciously sought her, but I could not understand how I had been so changed. I loved my wife, I was happy with our children, I enjoyed my job. I was writing a second novel and had every reason to believe it would be as successful as the first. I had taken a post at the University of Sydney; we lived in an elegant house in an area of smart, restrained terraces on tree-lined avenues near the ocean. I was content with life, to the extent of safeguarding the things which made me happy. Perhaps I feared that they were too fragile to withstand surprise.

I banged the door on the way out, to show my children how much they could hurt and tire us. It began over a promise made when we were still in Bogota, that if they did well enough at school in Australia they could spend the summer with school friends in Manaus. Now that we were in Australia they could not understand why it was almost impossible to keep the promise.

I did not have the patience to feel sorry for them. Their beautiful playroom, brimming with expensive toys, in the middle of ridiculously wealthy bourgeoisie, felt like whining in the lap of affluence. As my wife made me feel like a criminal, I compared my children's position with my own childhood, in the swamps of Manaus, either lashed by rain or licked by a mad and relentless sun. Eventually my son, his pugnacious face turned puce with indignation, forced out 'I hate you. I'm going to kill you', and sat on the floor of the serene room and proceeded to choke on his own bile while the teddies scampered around the wall.

I felt distant from it all. Outside, night fell among the immense jacarandas and settled its velvet wealth on the sleek Mercedes and vintage Citroens displaced from Europe. My daughter stood over me accusingly in her nightdress and my wife tucked her hair behind her ears and bent over our purpling son, giving me reproachful glances. I said something sarcastic about the terrible wealth we had forced our children to suffer, and left the house with a bang.

I walked about the streets for a bit and thought about how much I loved my wife. I remembered our student years at Bogota when we met, during a sit-in to protest some injustice to the Indians. I was the only one left sitting hours after the authorities had given in, lost in her buttery warm brown skin and all the peace beads braided into her shining hair.

On the unlit street I passed under immense trees, still dripping with rain, and thought how dissolving English-speaking countries are. There existed so many enchanting winds – the Tramontana, the Simoun, the Harmattan, the Mistral. But the constant wind which roared up from the harbour of Sydney, and the deep and fragrant darkness which fell unnoticed every night, remained nameless.

I wondered later, if the two women had changed places and I had seen my wife in the street instead of the girl - what would the effect have been on my life? Luisa belonged to a certain cadre of elegant and articulate women, whose effortless transition from peaceniks to slim well-kept cosmopolitans terrified me. Life seemed to come so easily to them. They accepted their value, their attraction, the idea that the world would compliantly fold itself around them.

I had been out for an hour. Another light rain began to fall on the canopy of trees. I approached a cafe on the corner, a steel and polished wood affair and had decided to go in when I saw her.

In itself it was not a shattering moment. She did not stop, and I spent nearly two years trying to realise that I had not existed for her, even in that brief moment. I was walking on an uneven stretch of pavement and did not see her approach, but when I looked up, she was there. A face swimming out of the darkness, a face of such charm, of so many questions and such beauty, the face of Neruda's Sirena, the hand in the dark of Chekhov's Kiss, the perfectly imperfect face which put writing to shame.

We looked at each other as we walked by, and in a second, years flashed past, my tongue strangled on my words, and I felt a fire in my bowels. My whole soul recognized her. Time slowed and I thought, 'There you are.' In the months which followed, when I was nearly fired from my job, when my children's whining in our beautiful house was at its shrillest and my wife's well-kept beauty at its most predictable, I would lock myself in the study and weep hot tears. I grieved the irrecoverable character of that moment, when all time and possibility was bottlenecked by the power of her face.

I came to understand hopelessness. It was accepting that I would never know the name of the woman who had become a muse, an intercessory saint.

I some part of me has remained there forever, inching closer along the dark street towards her pale face. She wore something dark, from which the loveliness of her face flowered like a light. She was quite young, perhaps only twenty, and I felt, as I came closer to her, the darkness stripping back the skins of my middle age, a green and truant hope well up. She had green eyes, I remember, and a hauteur which sat, like rank, in her mouth and nose. In her face was this entire new world, its unnamed winds and eucalypt forests, its blue harbour into which men had only lately and magically sailed. I think that I could only have found her here, in this strange and contradictory continent. I think I have thought too much about her. She is all I write now, having left me impotent to write anything else.

She turned her eyes away in a flicker of modesty which reminded me of *chansons des gestes*, of romances where the lady was a flower, and where there are opportunities which never flower. I stammered a greeting; she turned her eyes to me and I was washed away, and felt rain fall on my own dry soul.

Then she passed me by, swimming on through the night, alone and self-possessed, taking all the charm in the world with her.

I have never ceased to dream of her. There are many tales of brief encounters and of the wrecks left by them, on the sharp and invisible rocks which circle the sea of happiness. I have never finished my novel. My children went to Manaus, and returned, hard hearted and grasping as before. I put my hand over my wife's face as I sleep with her, and imagine the face of the swimmer in the darkness. I have written novels about her in my heart and found them all unfinished. I take my children to school along that street. Holding their hands, I understand that in the midst of brittle contentment there was a moment when, absently, I caught and lost the richest of perfumes. I do not know what happened that night, but a stranger took my soul from me as she passed by on the street, and now I am not the same.

Entropy

Emma flicked one end of the pencil and watched it spin, a yellow sun on the desk. 'Explain it again,' she commanded.

Nicholas leaned back in the chair, crossing his arms. He looked at her with some interest. It was a different kind of interest to the benign fondness he had tried to show her previously. This was partly because he was frustrated - explaining chemistry to a seventeen-year-old was not his forte - and partly because he was confused. The girl he had been seeing had cancelled dinner and he had been glad, though he couldn't have said why.

He picked up the textbook, thinking. Then he replaced it on the shelf. Why would she not meet his eyes? Why could he not meet hers? Something had changed between him and Emma, but he couldn't put his finger on what it was. This annoyed him, because he thought that he knew himself, and as for her, he had known her since the day she had been born, and someone who had faded from memory had laid the milk-smelling bundle of hot blankets in his nine-year-old's arms.

'What exactly don't you understand?' he said finally.

She stared mutinously ahead. 'All of it. What *is* a reaction anyway? And enthalpy and exogamy and-'

'Entropy.'

'Yes, *fine*. Entropy. What even are they? Mmm? I mean, what do they actually *do*?'

They had been at this all afternoon since he had foolishly offered to help with her Chemistry homework. Over the two hours since lunch he had noticed that she suddenly seemed to have cheekbones which weren't there before. And a distinct lower lip, full and firm, where there had only been a childish pucker. She had always had dangerous eyes; he remembered that from the earliest days. Absinthe, wicked green faery eyes, eyes to fall into, to be told lies by, eyes incapable of lying about herself.

'A reaction is just a change,' he said slowly. 'It just means breaking something up and doing different things with the bits. The cake in the textbook…'

She made an indescribable noise about the cake in the beleaguered textbook. 'Not exactly sexy, as examples go,' she said angrily. 'Maybe if the examples were a bit more exciting, they'd *mean* more.' She was looking fixedly at his mouth, but whether in interest or rage, he felt too dazed to say.

Suddenly, she looked into his eyes, then quickly away again. He felt as if a sparkler had been handed to him, burning a brief and furious energy. He got up and locked the door. She watched with an irate mid-afternoon apathy. 'Get up.'

She stood up, tugging at her hated school uniform. She stood before him, shirt untucked from skirt, one sock on, her tie hanging around her collar, undone.

'You're a chemical product,' he said, noticing that her eyes came level with his chest. He looked at the tangle of chestnut hair, remembering when it had been a shining bob level with his knee. Of that child there was no sign in the young woman before him.

'Alright,' she said suspiciously.

'You're a combination of a body,' putting a cool finger under her chin, 'and bits of clothing. Maybe a few atoms of lip gloss and earrings.'

Her lips twitched in a tiny smile. 'Everything that makes up this element - let's call it schoolgirlium –' she snorted at this, 'is held together with energy. So it's energy holding the gloss atoms to the lip atoms, the earing to the ear, the clothes to the body.'

'Mmmmhhmm,' she parted her lips a little as she hummed this. He saw a matchstick-thin line of darkness between her lips and wondered how the space of desire could be so small.

'So where's the reaction?' She was looking up at him now and wouldn't look away.

'Well, here,' he said. 'Imagine I'm a match.'

'A match?'

'A lit match, burning away the bonds between the atoms. Obviously, the most loosely attached things go first - the tie,' pulling it out of her collar, 'and the sock.' Both were thrown into the corner. 'Then the more firmly-attached things.'

He put two hands on her waist and slowly propelled her around, unzipped her skirt and watched it slide to the floor. She completed the revolution and faced him in her skirt and a pair of mummy-chosen Marks and Spencers knickers. She took her shirt collar in one hand. 'It's quite firmly attached.' She lifted a quizzical eyebrow and he realised how far and fast she had moved him away from the arms that had held the milk-smelling bundle of blankets.

'It's a very hot match,' he said, undoing her a little more. He was only slightly surprised that she was braless. Nothing that was happening that afternoon seemed to be happening in ordinary time. He sensed that fighting it would cause a kind of headache like sea-sickness. Going in the direction he was drawn, however, felt as though he were on the brink of a singularity, with light and time being devoured.

She stood naked, pearlescent and suddenly, almost terrifyingly, adult. So Zeus must have felt, he thought, when Athena appeared fully grown.

'What about the other atoms?' she said, leaning towards him. He grasped her upper arms and drew her into a kiss. He leaned back on the flimsy desk in her bedroom, bringing her own head towards his. There was still something troubling in their different heights and how he towered over her. It struck him that he probably always would.

She broke a kiss that came entirely without awkwardness, and with a certain familiarity that inspired dread in him. 'So you burned away the bonds,' she said. 'And then?'

He gestured to the pile of clothes. 'The products,' he said. 'A pile of clothes and a naked girl. The bonds have been turned into.... well, let's call it environmental heat.'

She snorted again and gave a laugh. 'If that's enthalpy, what's entropy?' She sat on the desk, swinging long pale legs, tugging him around to face her.

'Remember the golf-ball pyramid in the textbook?'

'Mmm.'

'It had low entropy – think of it as tidiness. Entropy's just another word for chaos. When you're tidy, there's not much chance of a reaction.'

'But when my…'

'Atoms.'

'Yes, thank you, *atoms* are in a mess, a reaction's more likely?'

He took her hands in his. 'Sometimes you simply see a pyramid of girls, all neatly put together and indistinguishable. It's like looking at a school photograph. Just hundreds of faces packed in. Then the bell rings, the atoms go flying, and one comes towards you and in the chaos a reaction happens.'

She looked at their joined hands and twined her bare legs around him. She tugged at his belt and flicked one end free. He felt his heart, thudding in his chest, begin to race. 'I was right,' she said happily. 'A sexier example makes it all clear.'

'Really.' The rattle of the buckle sounded loudly in the stillness of her room. He admitted to himself that he was glad she had demanded they come home rather than going out for tea.

'Really. And now that you've burned the bonds, there's only one bit left to do.'

'What's that?'

She lay back on the desk, like butter shortbread in the four o'clock sunlight of half term. 'Split the atom.'

Maze

'You've *got* to come,' Nikolai said. 'Uncle William's making me do it, and I can't do it without you.'

He looked at me with plangent blue eyes and I nearly gave in. He meant the maze, of course; Uncle William had said that when the great maze had fully regrown, and we all came back to Wilton for the summer, there would be a prize for the first to reach the centre. Cecilia and her twin Francis were not interested in the maze; my older sister Elizabeth refused to try it, citing fear of small spaces and intellectual challenges, and the Amberley cousins Thomas, Michael, and Ninette were busy trying to persuade Uncle William to open the gardens to the public. That left Nicky and I, the oldest and youngest of the cousins respectively.

'I want to finish my book,' I said uncomfortably. In the year since I had seen him, Nikolai had become annoyingly handsome and now my feelings for him bothered me. We were third cousins – by marriage, so there was no blood relation – but I was the shortest, chubbiest, youngest, and … most plainly British of all the exotic cousins. Nikolai, with his crown of dark brown hair and blue eyes, his superman kiss-curl and height, had been the delightful torment of Christmases, summers, and Easters while I was at school. He probably didn't want me to go, I told myself, he just needed my sense of direction. Although clever in many ways – he had just taken a first in Russian – Nicky could be unbelievably stupid in others. He still got lost in Uncle William's vast Henrician pile and had spent nights sleeping in spare rooms when he couldn't find his own. He had no idea what to do with his life and – unpardonably, in our large, successful, and mendacious family – was doing a bad job of concealing his confusion. I overheard Uncle William telling him to go and find himself, in an ashram if he had to.

I went off to finish my book – it was *Jane Eyre*, for the hundredth time – and lose myself in that terrific scene of wordless passion where Jane saves brooding, morally dubious Rochester (whom I always imagined with dark hair and blue eyes and a Russian dictionary in one hand) from being burnt alive in his bed. Alone, soaking wet (from the pitcher of water Jane has upended over him), and deeply frustrated in the dead of night, Rochester shakes Jane's hand in gratitude. And that's it. But that handshake, in which everything and nothing is said, is still one of the hottest damn pieces of literature yet.

Nicky passed the oak tree under which I sat and paused. 'If I'm not back by dusk, you'll *have* to come and get me. And the prize.'

I waved him on. 'You'll be fine. Dusk's hours away yet.'

'I'm counting on you to rescue me.' He smiled, and I saw myself reflected in his eyes – a doughy bundle beneath the tree, clutching my fat little knees and my book. I looked like a gnome, I thought.

He vanished into the maze. I fell asleep before I got to the bed-burning chapter.

Two hours later the sun was low in the sky. The roses beneath the south drawing room window were releasing a heavy perfume into the air. I was nearly at the bed burning bit, and Nicky still hadn't emerged from the maze.

I put the book down and wondered if I should go after him. Maybe he was in the middle already with Uncle William's prize, whatever it was. Or hopelessly lost again, getting tired and hungry and panicking as even the most sensible do when they admit that they're alone, trapped, disoriented. I couldn't decide whether he had really meant it when he asked me to come. How could someone like that want me? How could he want to be rescued by me?

Nowadays we're not supposed to rescue each other. We're all supposed to be responsible, resilient, forward-oriented. I had spent six years at a girls' school where capable, intelligent women took a stern view of girls who wanted to be rescued by men. They were at pains to explode the handsome-prince myth. What I took from it was that the general demands on people now were extremely high, and people-as-romantic-prospects even more so. *You can't expect anyone to like you if you don't like yourself.* All that stuff about being your own best friend first. Making something of yourself before deciding with whom and how to share it. Being, I realised, Jane to the world's Rochester.

When we rescue someone we expose so much of ourselves. We say *I missed you. I feared for you, even here, even on a summer evening. I came for you. I am strong enough to carry you back, if need be.* And for their part, they must bear being rescued with good grace. Even the handsome, the clever, the grown up.

Were we like that? Could I let Nicky know that I was here, fearing for him, thinking of him? I quailed at the thought of being laughed at, thrown back on my books.

I picked up Jane and Rochester again. A slump in the pages showed that a chapter had been neatly excised with a sharp blade. The burning bed scene was gone. In its place, written in Nicky's neat script on the next chapter heading were the words: *I'm lost. Find me.*

I stared at the page for a moment, then put down the book. I went into the maze, which was now full of shadows, cold and needle-walled. The sun had sunk beneath the height of the privet walls, which had grown tall over the years of our childhood, while the maze had been closed. I walked on in the deepening gloom, the smell of earth exhaling loam and heat, faint tendrils of rose perfume drifting over it all.

The centre is never very hard to find when it's all you're looking for. There, in the little clearing by the vine-covered statue of Diana, was my oldest cousin, his arms open and waiting for me. We had both found our prize.

Vellum

A man came into a shop one afternoon in the heat and dust. Bullock carts went by and stockmen shouted. A crow landed on the gable, while behind the shop snows fell on the efforts of the man from Snowy River. Everyone who went into the shop sought the same thing: paper on which to capture the Pacific blue glimpsed among the harbour's rolling inlets and wooded, forgotten slopes.

Accountants came looking for three-column cashbooks of perfect pulp which would account for the cerulean sky, the sun shining bright on the shore. Typewriter-girls came looking for the thinnest translucent paper on which to beat the scent of eucaplyt and the shadows of men prospecting for dreams between the shocking white blanks. Their tiny steel hammers beat poems to the perfection of Gondwanaland.

Poets came looking for parchment which crumpled and writhed in paper rivers from their tears. Cartographers sought graph paper on which to chart the forgotten routes of the Antipodean shade, the hidden trails in the elbow of navigation lines.

The only imam on the whole great island came looking for a sheet on which to inscribe letters which resembled the rivers and mountains and the fabulous birdcalls of the most discreet continent, because images were forbidden to him.

The shop girl found paper for them all, even lovers found the likeness of their beloved's skin lodged in the drawers of the paper shop. Evan's hard hands and King's white ones, Cook's pointing finger and the scorched texture of Baudin's back, burnt by the eyes of those who watched him sail into forgotten pockets and terrifying pagan corners of the globe; they all found their own touch in the paper's scented susurrations.

She was an expert in guessing the true nature of the buyer and the paper appropriate to each. While it may have seemed an unsatisfactory mistake at the time, bankers became poets and stockmen politicians, while famers and graziers discovered riverbeds their wives' hands, all thanks to a slip of paper selected for them.

One day a man came in requesting a perfectly virginal sheet of paper; one which never known the sweat of loggers and lumberjacks or the sadness of commercial forests.

She looked at the man's hands and saw that he had touched everything, beginning with absolute purity and ending in a degradation of touch which barely felt anything. His eyes were of the deepest blue and had looked on every sight without surprise. His was the heat of the ocean on islands orbiting islands, the stage-curtain heavy heat of equatorial archipelagos.

This man, who had arrived at the ends of the world on a boat named Amnesia, wanted to write about his wandering and the awful inconclusiveness which he suffered and then to let a kind of insomnia take him.

He saw only a dark girl with the green eyes of jungles and curved, smooth brows about to tell him that there was not a single scrap of paper in the world which could bear his story without returning to rags. But she, taking him by the hand to a back room, loosened her hair and, baring her neck, invited him to hang his life in words around her throat.

She pointed to a brown mark above and between her breasts (as though she had been touched lightly by the tip of a finger, only once, and had been more truly marked by that than any other touch in her life), and she indicated that his tale should reach this far, and no further.

And indeed, his life stretched from the white, soft skin where her hair crept from the nape of her neck, around her throat, under her silent mouth. It dipped into the damp honey between her collarbones and recounted the sweat of deserts and of drowned ships, whirlpools and the drowsy happiness of a filled wadi.

And he reached the spot on her breast and ended there, happy and relieved that his story had coextended with her skin.

Contracted

They were married in the little church at Holmbury St Mary; the vicar took the Aretino triptych out of its wrappings, gritty with dust and glass from the bomb which had struck the north chapel. William did not wear his uniform. His morning dress made him look smaller, older, and more of the Foreign Office. Her parents left immediately after the wedding breakfast because her mother wanted to return home to feed the twins, whom the family agreed were the only good surprise presented by the war. Deborah did not ask them to stay because she couldn't honestly say that she wanted them to.

She was well aware that this – being unable to say something honestly – was how she had ended up married. Since she had no real preferences about anything, it seemed natural that people who did have preferences should take precedence. Her parents said that her lack of inclination for anything was just a well-disguised laziness or immaturity. They did not seem particularly dismayed about this. Deborah wondered if this would have been different had she been a boy. When William, fifteen years her senior and going to a diplomatic posting in Morocco, said she should marry him, she couldn't find a reason to object. She was nineteen, unsuitable for a job, and William wanted her. She waved her parents off from the hotel doorway, feeling forlorn in her taffeta, still clutching the tulips that her mother had wanted for the bouquet.

They muddled through a wedding night which satisfied what William wanted. She lay still, feeling formless and soggy, while William arranged himself for sleep. It surprised her that such fuss was made about an act which had no definite beginnings and such a laughable ending. When they arrived at the embassy's married quarters in Rabat, she was told to arrange the house in any way that suited her. She left everything as William had put it. He arranged French lessons to supplement her schoolgirl French, but she found Darija easier and more interesting - even if it had to be learned surreptitiously. William had no Darija, and no intention of learning it. He read French well enough, if the books on his bedside were anything to go by. He was reading a book called *L'histoire de l'œil* by Georges Bataille. She thought it was about optometry until she read the opening vignette. William came in while she was struggling with an adjective that she realized meant *starched*.

'Do you want to read it?', he said, sitting on the bed.

'Is it good?'

He laughed. 'That's not a word associated with this book.'

'Then why are you reading it?'

He gave a small smile, which he quickly swallowed. It was not a look which she had seen before; not a disposition she associated with William. 'Has it occurred to you that I might not be good?'

She realized that William's moral character had never crossed her mind. It was not that she believed that she would end up with a good person, as her parents clearly assumed. Or that she was entitled to it, as her sister had. Contrary to the prevailing belief in Surrey during the war, goodness seemed to require choices, which in turn required knowing what you wanted. Without the boulders of intended action or desires, life flowed around and through you, she thought, and you were carried away down a peaceful stream.

'I hadn't thought about that.'

He got into bed. 'I've never known how you do it,' he said, 'this...passivity. It seems unhealthy to be so, I don't know, still.' He took her hand and looked at her speculatively as she stood by the bed, holding the book. 'Still, never look a gift horse in the mouth.'

She got into her own side of the bed and went to sleep.'

*

Now, at the gate of the Souk el-Attarine William again takes her hand and brings something out of his pocket. She stands in silence as the women - all a head and shoulders shorter than she in her espadrilles - flow past her. She thinks it might be nice to roam through the perfume market alone, just for a little while, but it seems rude to push William away now and ask if he hasn't some embassy business to get on with.

He is unwinding a small skein of red thread - her own embroidery thread, she sees - and tying it in a loop with a complicated knot around the little finger of her left hand. 'What on earth are you doing?'

'Making sure I don't lose you,' he says, tying the other end around his own thumb. 'Darling.'

'You're joking,' she says. She feels a kind of lurch in her stomach. 'I'm not a dog. William!' But he has proceeded into the market, and when a foot and a half of red thread has played out, she is tugged along on his heels.

He spends a few moments looking at a small spice-grinder, asking the man how much he wants for it, while she struggles vainly with the loop of silk. It tightens as she tugs at it. She realizes that William is giving her a minute to exhaust herself with the fetter, the way you allow a young dog to half-strangle itself with a lead before it gives up and walks at heel. The spice-seller either does not notice or does not see anything strange about the young white woman in a white blouse and blue skirt and hat pulling at the red circle on her little finger.

William puts down the grinder and walks away, drawing her with him. 'Ma salitsh!' The man calls after them. *I'm not finished.*

'Mashi dabia,' she mouths at him. *Not now.* 'Are you angry with me about something?'

He turns slightly. 'Of course not. I just don't want you to get lost here, that's all.'

'What about what I want?'

He laughs. 'You're always saying you don't know what you want. North Africa's a dangerous place when you don't know what you want.'

'I don't want this,' she says. She has the sense that she should be more outraged, but that outrage - even the fear that she suspected she should feel - was foreign to her. 'It's perverse and ridiculous. Take it off, William. Please.'

But he turns and again the swarm of bodies parts and flows around them; the red thread becomes invisible in the flux of djellabas and bundles of goods, and she is tugged along like a puppet, or a bee drawn drunkenly to the next flower. She tries to see if anyone else is thus constrained, but it is impossible to see beneath djellaba sleeves, and Moroccan couples do not shop together.

She closes the gap between them but a feeling of dislike prevents her from putting a hand on his blue-blazered shoulder. She realizes, with a dull surprise like the aftermath of a bee-sting, that she does not like her husband. The smell of rose-attar, leather and heavy cotton accompanies this thought. She looks around for someone, a woman, to whom she can mouth *Awni afak*, but no one will look at them in the souk's winding whitewashed passage. Anyway, what help could they give her against her own husband? Even if she were in Holmbury St Mary, how could anyone help her against the man she has so lately, apparently, chosen?

'William, you don't *tie* your wife to you in a public place.' She says this mostly to his blue-banded panama, beneath which she can see a fringe of thinning sandy hair. She thinks that she has never touched his hair, nor does she want to. Ever, she realizes.

'No one here would think twice about doing it if he was with his wife in Piccadilly Circus.'

They are halfway down the long passage of the souk when the call to afternoon prayer filters through the stalls. There is a discernable shift, as stallholders begin to retire to back rooms, flap out sellayas, and turn away from the white couple walking in single file along the cobbles. As the passage empties and the red thread surfaces from the flux of bodies which has obscured it, a number of things coalesce in her mind. One is that she does not want to be alone with her husband. A second is that William does not seem to be her husband. A third is that she wants to leave the confines of the souk, to go and not to return. She does not want to be in England, or in the house in Rabat - full of William's things, his books, his strange looks, the silences before bedtime. It will take some time to arrive at what she wants, and now she is ready to accept the task of spending that time.

It occurs to her that William might be doing this as a joke, a game. Perhaps it is sexual, in some way. She turns this thought around and considers it, as he continues walking along the souk-passage, forcing her to toddle in his wake. She decides that she does not care whether it is a joke. She is no longer interested in William, or his intentions, or what he might find amusing. She is interested in herself, and the fact that, suddenly, almost incredibly, she has a distinct and urgent preference for something.

She creates some slack in the red thread, then bends her head to it and takes it in her teeth.

Gaze

My mother had a painful fear of people looking. 'For goodness' sake,' she would hiss when any of us did something mildly unusual, 'people are *looking*.' Then she would draw her cardigan or coat around herself more tightly, as if it were a cloak of invisibility, and bustle off down the street at a speed designed to stay just ahead of the looking.

None of us ever worked out whether anyone actually *was* looking, or if they were, what they did about whatever they saw. We just accepted it as one of our mother's peculiarities and tried to be inconspicuous for her sake. My two younger siblings were largely unscathed by it; Jenny even became a dance teacher, an occupation based on inculcating the desire to be looked at. We all moved far enough away from Mother to be able to enjoy graduations, weddings, and houses painted pale pink. (This was Richard's, which he explained as the perfect colour for a seaside home, but I think it was mostly to lay to rest mother's oft-repeated belief that anything but weathered sandstone would make people *look*).

As the eldest, I expect I bore the brunt of Mother's obsession with avoiding attention. It didn't harm me in any measurable way; she expected me to do well in school and was pleased when I achieved to distinction, but this was, somehow, different to the business of drawing attention. The net result was that I could come top of my year but would have to forgo prizegiving.

Fortunately, as I grew up it turned out that I wasn't much to look at anyway, but I saw friends' mothers push them forward, showing them how to be prettier, to catch the eye or, as Jane Austen would have put it, dispose themselves to appear to distinction. But our mother resisted the urge to help us along in the looks department, even when it became clear that Richard was going to turn out so disgustingly handsome that he made girls turn and point in the street.

I got used to sidling along the pavement, bundling myself into myself, like an envelope with curled edges. I usually sat on the outskirts of any room, and never wore anything that could have been called eye-catching. In a way, it was a nice, quiet little life and mother would have been happy.

Of course life, like a high street bank, tends to return the most grudging interest for the shortest time it can, and it's only by making significant investments that you can tug the balance of the whole machine to work for you. I found that work, my siblings, a few friends and staying healthy kept me quite busy enough. Any extra interest wasn't expected.

So when I began it feel the desire to be looked at, it weighed heavily on me. I noticed him the first time when I got up in the night to get a glass of water. It was hot and, although technically still night, you could feel the dawn buzzing just gently in the air, like a lot of kids whispering behind a stage curtain. I stood in the kitchen, feeling the floor cool under my feet, looking out the window to the quiet street below.

He was leaning against a low brick wall, long legs crossed at the ankle, his arms folded over his chest. I've seen joggers out that early, and a few dog walkers, even people doing the early-hours walk of shame, with smudgy mascara and shoes in hand. But never anyone looking up at the kitchen window, leaning on a wall in the silent street, as if all he expected to see was a girl in the dark glass square, with a silver glass of water in her hand.

I couldn't see his face clearly. I looked out for a moment at him – it's funny how time, in the dark, when everyone else is at the deepest point of sleep, stretches out. And any act, as long as it's said or done in the tempo of those long, quiet hours, seems permissible. I went back to bed.

It occurred to me, later in the morning, that it was probably the first time in my life that I'd been properly looked at. And that my mother, had it happened to her, would have reacted entirely differently. She would have drawn back like a whippet, yanked down the blind and checked the deadlock on the front door. Then I thought that I was glad I wasn't my mother. I had enjoyed being looked at. It had done me good somehow, the way a hearty meal or a well-earned rest does you good.

I see him sometimes, in the street, watching the window. I've never seen his face, clearly, and I'm not sure that I want to. I think he may watch me at other times. I feel him just behind me sometimes. Or rather, I feel his gaze. That's what I enjoy most, the protective bubble of his gaze. We have discovered each other, and I think we do each other good somehow. We need to see and to be seen, to be completely sure that we actually exist. His are the eyes that make the I, if that's not being clever.

Perhaps you think I should be worried. He's a stalker and I'm lonely. It's the worst combination in the world. But he's never done me any harm, and I've never felt endangered. Should I want to drop, unnoticed, undiscovered, off the edge of the human map, like my mother? No thanks. I don't want to be a whole continent for the colonizing gaze of rapacious millions. Just a quiet corner, some sun and shade, a flower or two, where I can look and be looked at, and know that I'm here.

Housework

The boys wore open bathrobes and striped shorts. Sarah watched them from the kitchen window. They ran down the quarter mile of rear lawn and along the jetty, stripping off the robes as they went, before bombing into the Sound. Mr. Winthrop's yacht bobbed and twisted in the turbulence like a lady trying to make her way in a crowd. She hoped the boys wouldn't try to climb onto the yacht. Mr. Winthrop had instructed her to telephone him and then the police if his son or any of his son's friends attempted brigandage with the *Lara*.

She counted only five sleek short-back-and-sides in the water. That probably meant that the Etherton boy, Cordell, was still asleep in the house somewhere. She sighed and got started on the crystal, of which there wasn't too much. Despite glasses being available, most of Master David's friends drank beer from a bottle. She shook her head at the thought of Cordell Etherton hungover and passed out somewhere in the house. He had been a handsome boy, more than any of the others, she thought, but there was a weakness, a recklessness, that was showing itself now in drinking. The flowering chestnut by the front gates had been removed – the stump ground right down so it wouldn't regrow and another sapling planted in its place – after he had driven his car into it while drunk. Mr Winthrop had been furious.

Sarah dried the last glass and set it on the table. Before noon the house had to be set to rights, those of the family provided with breakfast and bloody marys, those not of the family woken, re-clothed, en-taxied and sent home. Any losses had to be made good and damage fixed either by her own efforts of those of whatever tradesman Master David would pay for.

She took off her apron and went into the passage between her world and the upper realm of the Winthrops – heavy curtains, oak panelling, automobile money and thin brittle women in good clothes. Already she could hear the sound of someone being copiously sick.

The ballroom was in surprisingly respectable order. Two girls lay curled on the Louis quinze sofas in clouds of tulle and chiffon, like dolls only half-unpacked. Gloved hands under their cheeks had prevented face-powder stains on the upholstery. They snuffled like puppies as she passed, cutting off the early sunlight that struck their faces and reflected the soft deep glow of money.

Cordell Etherton was not the source of the vomiting sound. He lay asleep beneath the billiards table, which was mercifully unripped, and all the cues whole. She made a mental note to wake him last. She had learned from painful experience that it was better to let sleeping millionaires' sons lie. She had woken him once and found him still in the fighting mood from the last drink. He had swung wildly, caught her eye, and then laughed at the small likelihood of her black skin showing the bruise. Mr Winthrop had apologized for his son's guest's behaviour. His atonement had paid for Tony's first year of tuition at Hampton, but she had wept and wept at the greater deficit that money could not cover.

She saw that the door to Mr Winthrop's study was ajar. It shouldn't have been; it was a private room – only Robert cleaned it and only he brought Mr Winthrop drinks and (when Mrs Winthrop was away) dinner in there. Hesitantly, she looked around the padded door. A girl sat on the sofa in her slip. Her dress was a crumped pile of gauzy pink beneath the window. From the door, she could smell expensively old brandy. The girl's arms were on her knees, her head hanging its tumble of Hamptons-blonde curls around her shoulders. A diamond earring peeped from one ear. Fuchsia bruises, in mans-hand patterns, sprinkled her arms and shoulders. Her wrist still bore a corsage of withered stephanotis.

Sarah cleared her throat in the doorway. The girl looked up. The Hamilton girl, Sarah thought. Evie? No, that was the older one. Adeline. Not one of the giddy ones, but not a wallflower either.

71

Another of the serried ranks of radiant blondes that kept her employed in the in-between spaces of their vast houses. She went to the window and picked up the dress, shaking out the folds and layers. There was a brownish smear on the back of the inside layer. It wouldn't show from the outside – it never did – but it showed that Addie Hamilton had been demoted to second-rank Newport.

The girl looked at Sarah, looking at the dress. She made a helpless gesture and winced as she moved her bruised arms. 'I don't even know…who,' she said. She hung her head and began to cry. Softly, hopelessly, decoratively, even then.

Sarah draped the dress over the back of the sofa. The only boy brave enough to trespass in the study was Master David himself. She thought about the implications of saying this. Tony had another two years of college and she had counted on working until she was too old to need anyone. Her plan had always been to die in harness; to see Tony off to college and a good job and to keep going, being a burden to no one. Besides, until this she had never thought David a bad boy. Stupid, outside his own rarefied world, but no worse than the rest of them.

She put a tentative hand on the girl's shoulder to comfort her. The shoulder froze, tightened, and shook off her hand. 'Don't touch me.'

Sarah withdrew her hand and stood for a long moment, smelling the rich, alcohol-drenched perfume of the study. She bent down and picked up a glass, rolling on its side beneath the sofa beside a hairclip and some of the browned stephanotis blooms from the corsage. She opened the curtains and straightened the decanters reminding herself that the rug would have to be removed and sent for cleaning. It was Persian and could only be done by a specialist. She put the clip on the table and took the glass away for washing.

On her way back through the billiards room she bent down beneath the table. Cordell was now snoring lightly. She strewed a few of the dead stephanotis blooms by his head and put a few more, still pungent with fragrance, in the pocket of his tuxedo. Then she began prodding him with her toe, telling him to wake up and do some explaining about the state of Miss Hamilton.

Makeover

It was Trinny and Susannah, that horrible pair of southern English women who bullied and cajoled what they clearly saw as their social inferiors into stylishness, who pointed out that no woman is sexy in a cardigan. I remember turning to David (in my blue cardigan, with holes in the pockets where the seedlings sometimes fell through when I was gardening) and said, 'Is that true?'

He shrugged. 'I've never thought about it.'

I also remember thinking that I should leave him alone. It was after seven and he'd had a hard day. I had a mortal fear of hen-pecking him, or sounding like one of those whiny, needy women who want reassured about their attractiveness every other day. But I wore cardigans with everything. I'd trained as a teacher and been in the classroom for a few years until David persuaded me – or did I persuade myself? – that I'd enjoy life more at home. I brought the cardigans from the classroom with me.

I persisted. 'I suppose that means I'm not sexy. I mean, if I wear a cardigan with everything – and I do – then I'm always un-sexy.'

What did I want to hear? I wasn't sure, exactly. In fact, as I said it, I realized that I already knew what he'd say, and that I was only saying it for confirmation. He looked bored and stared at the television. 'Then stop wearing cardigans.'

'Would that make me sexy to you?' The word *sexy* just sounded all wrong in our living room. It hung in the air and rubbed up wrongly against the neat curtains, the French doors, the sofa, and us, sitting on a three-seater sofa with the middle cushion occupied by two china mugs and polite plate of post-tea biscuits.

'What?'

'Sexy. Would it make me sexy if I stopped wearing cardigans?'

He patted my hand without looking at me. 'You watch these ridiculous shows and get insecure. I can't understand why you do it to yourself.'

And that was that.

That had been a full six months before. We didn't fight about it. We didn't fight about anything. No, he wasn't having an affair, and I didn't go off and have a wild makeover to inject something back into our marriage. It just came to me, over the course of months that not only did we barely know each other, but that we actually nursed a healthy dislike for each other. Not hatred, but the way you begin to stare with dislike at the back of someone ahead of you in a queue, taking too long.

I still factored David in to even the smallest decision, making sure I'd be at home with dinner ready when he came back from work, but I discovered that for twenty years – twenty years, I thought! Where has it gone and with what else could I have filled it except this strange, muffled life, of pottering and tinkering, popping out and nipping in? – I'd operated mostly on autopilot.

David worked as an insurance actuary and if I had once known what that involved, I had long forgotten. He took three weeks off each July and we went to a cottage in the Hebrides, where he also went with his brother for a week in April and another week in September, ostensibly to fish, but probably to lie around and enjoy wife-less peace and quiet. We didn't have children; neither of us liked noise, chaos, mess and demanding behaviour. We had one extremely sour old cat called Tink, who treated us like flatmates. And that was all. I had a garden, a large collection of books, and some middle-aged-lady ideas of one day writing a novel.

Sadly, I also had a horrible case of writer's block. I had lost the habit of trying, and risking, and producing, that work demands. By work, I mean paid work, where you're exposing your soft underbelly to other people all the time. Still, it ate at me, when I read the thin, pulpy rubbish that other women my age wrote. Women just like me,

I thought when I saw their stuff in bookshops, tasteful and sensitive and mostly forgettable.

Every so often I would try to write something, fail miserably, pack it all up and then make David a lavish and beautiful dinner served in a frighteningly-clean dining room. For the next few weeks I would pour everything I had into him, as if trying to make him as sleek and glossy as a well-fed tomcat would replace the harder work I was too lazy to try for.

The more I considered it, the more surprised I grew at how long this absence from my own life had gone on, and how little David had noticed it. He asked dutifully every evening what I'd done that day, and not once had he ever said that the repeated potterings, tinkering, and so on sounded like a rather feckless life propped up by a vocabulary of harmlessness.

'Do you mind that I don't work?'

He looked up over the paper. 'No, why should I?'

'I don't know. I thought that maybe you'd think I was wasting my time, my talent.' He had the good grace not to say, 'What talent?' but the words could have been printed on his face.

When he left for work that morning I began a thorough tidy of the house, more thorough than I'd done since we bought it ten years before. I suppose I wanted to make a pile of *things* with which to explain to myself where twenty years had gone.

I even tidied his study, not because I wanted to snoop, but because I simply wanted to see how far through my little domain lost time had extended.

I was running the vacuum over the carpet when it banged the desk and woke his computer up. Normally I'd have ignored his computer, but the page it woke up to, a screen full of text, caught my eye. Working in insurance meant that David mostly seemed to deal with graphs and spreadsheets. And if it wasn't insurance, it was fishing.

I read the text on the screen. It was an extract from a novel. A good novel, I decided. A philosophical novel, with a man and a woman in the middle of some ferry journey. I turned off the vacuum and sat at his desk. I scrolled to the beginning of the document.

It was titled *Hebridean Years* by David Sellars.

I spent the afternoon reading the first chapter. It was, quite simply, brilliant. A beautiful, thoughtful work about aging and the sadness of poor choices recognized too late. Phrases of which I would never have believed him capable appeared on page after page, the writing voice of a man I clearly never knew.

It may seem strange that I got angrier and angrier the longer I read, but you cannot judge until you've wasted twenty years caring for a man who, it turns out, has given you the scrag end of his time, his mind, his regard. I was the one who should have written the book, not desk-bound David the dullard.

The afternoon had disappeared and was turning into early evening when I stopped. Guiltily, I realized that I had no idea where he'd left the document. The wretched story was so fluidly written that I couldn't remember where I'd begun it.

When the doorbell rang I must have jumped like a guilty thing. I ran downstairs with my excuses at the ready. I wasn't ready to tell him that I'd read the novel yet; I wanted to plot out my position, decide how best to use the knowledge. I was only mildly surprised when I opened the door to two young constables who wore the anxious look of ill-news bearers.

'Mrs Sellars?'

'Yes.'

'Could we come in please? I'm afraid…I'm afraid there's been an accident.'

Part of me expected them to say that David had banged the car into something again. He'd done it twice before and freely admitted that it was because his mind was on other things.

It turned out that something had banged itself into David. He'd been caught by a truck at an intersection near the station car park, and killed instantly. I was trying to shuffle the discoveries of the afternoon into an orderly deck. The younger constable, a fair-haired boy young enough to be my son, said sadly, 'I'm so sorry to bring this, just…there you are, getting along with your day, putting the dinner on, when we have to tell you this.' He shook his head.

I patted his knee gently, feeling things drop into place. 'No, no,' I said. 'I was just writing.'

Not far from the tree

I once read that no man can watch a woman eating a banana without sniggering. Reverend Matheson couldn't watch anyone eating an apple without weeping inwardly at the memory of the fall. In the Matheson manse (airy, gloomy, and eternally smelling of Bizzy Bee furniture polish) apples were always cut into anonymous chunks. Madeleine, the youngest daughter, once had the misfortune to admire another child's dress, a frothy thing covered in tiny, shining red and green apples with sprigs of leaves and tiny twigs. Her father gave her the first of many deep gazes of disappointment.

Naturally, Hallowe'en was also uncelebrated in that household. On a street full of Jack o'lanterns, plastic skeletons, crepe-paper ghouls and ghosties, the manse remained serene, dour and unvisited by trick-or-treaters. Nobody minded - the consistency was valued; the manse had never celebrated Hallowe'en and that was as much part of the festival as all the rest.

Around September, in the year of Madeleine's Sweet Sixteen, the Reverend was asked to stand in for a sick colleague in his parish a whole state away. He would be away for the two weeks and return on All Hallows Day, the Monday after Hallowe'en. He was a good man; he loved his wife and five children, but he was secretly relieved to be going to the country for Hallowe'en. Sin prevaricated less in the country. It had a blunter aspect and fewer wordy excuses fuelled by weekend newspapers, and no one in the country had the money to waste on Hallowe'en trash.

'So you can come to my party,' Isabella Holland said, over their packed lunches.

Madeleine looked at her friend with the same apprehension Lilith must have felt for the Jinn.

'Come as something really good,' said Bella, eyeing Maddy's long, sinuous curves and wondering if she could tolerate a life of repression and denial if it produced such results. 'Come as something *not* from the Bible.' As her mother's Sunday School assistant, poor Maddy had been everything from a Nativity sheep to a tumbling block from the wall of Jericho.

'What about the Apocrypha?' said Maddy. She rather fancied herself wearing a sword and carrying around a head of Holofernes.

'Is that a superhero? Look, don't be stupid. Come as, like, I dunno...as a witch or something. A really sexy witch.'

'No, not a witch. There'll be loads there. I'll think about it. It'll be a surprise.'

Bella considered her friend suspiciously. 'Whatever. Just no god-bothering stuff. You've got so much potential. Don't waste it on that.'

Mrs Matheson often counted the days of her service to the Lord. In tasteful nightgowns and motherly dressing gowns she slid out of bed, weighed herself, made breakfast, and received her husband back from his dawn run, while reminding herself that thirty-two years as a minister's wife was an achievement that, like superannuation and a low sodium diet, would eventually pay dividends. Not something to be withdrawn from before the investment matured.

She had been, and still was when they needed the money, a primary school teacher. She lived with many subtle reminders that she was far less clever than her husband, but also far better at showing her children that she loved them. It seemed wrong, somehow, to ask children to connect punishments and moral remonstrations with parental love. They weren't machines of deductive reasoning. They were made for games and fun, cuddles and stories and sneaked treats at bedtime.

It was quite clear that Maddy was planning to go to the Holland girl's Hallowe'en party. She knew it, and Maddy knew that she knew it. Neither of them said anything, and Mrs Matheson turned a blind eye when her make up brushes disappeared and reappeared on Maddy's dresser and two old pairs of green nylon stockings (from a brief Princess Di phase shortly after Maddy had been born) also vanished and the snipped off toes appeared in the bathroom bin.

It was pleasant, thought mother and daughter, separately and in silence, to have a secret. Especially when it involved a party and dressing up, make-believe and harmless magic. Mrs Matheson didn't think about magic - she still remembered vividly a sermon her husband had preached some twenty years before, about the exhortation not to suffer a witch to live. She knew that the world turns, and what was once of the past and unthinkable comes around again and is inescapable.

They both paused at the pumpkins in the supermarket and fingered the slithery black binliners thoughtfully when they took out the trash. Maddy bought a new palette of green-blue eyeshadow under her mother's gaze when they were in the chemist, replacing her father's knee supports. 'New colour?' said her mother.

'I thought I'd try something different,' her daughter said, who was allowed makeup at weekends, and only inasmuch as it promoted a softer, more womanly appearance conducive to a godly marriage.

'Maybe I will too,' her mother said suddenly, placing a new frosted pink lipstick beside the flesh-coloured knee supports.

Mother and daughter knew that there was no possibility of Maddy's asking to attend the party. The most convenient way around the problem was for Mrs Matheson to read the Bible passage (which her husband usually did nightly for the assembled family) a little earlier and accept Maddy's explanation that she felt a headache coming on and would go to bed early. Her daughter was long limbed and light boned, and would face no danger in descending the lime tree in the garden.

As Mrs Matheson was fumbling with the purple ribbon - worn by her eldest daughter at her wedding - which marked the pericope for the evening, her husband was standing among the stale baked goods of the day and the imperishable confectionary, ordering a strong coffee at a freeway service station on his return journey. The sheer lack of sin in his colleague's parish had been initially cheering but two sleepy weeks convinced him that the rockier soil and tares of his own parish were worthier of his time. He preached, packed, and was on the freeway before midday.

Her husband always used the same pericope for Hallowe'en: Deuteronomy 18:10-13 with a chaser of Hebrews 10:27. It broke the lyrical continuity of their normal October reading (Esther and part of Daniel) but it was important. When she closed the book and stared softly at her infant son's slumbering face, she felt that she had done her duty by everyone, herself included.

She turned the television up and so missed the muffled thump from the back garden, and she was sure that the fleeing shadow by the gate was only the first of the evening's many floating trick-or-treaters. But she did remember to move the ladder from the shed and place it against the tree - the shed was close to the street and the ladder had been expensive. It would be unfortunate if a Hallowe'en prankster stole it. But it would be quite safe by the lime tree. Under Maddy's window.

As her father shook the drops from the petrol pump and retrieved his credit card, Maddy was a street away from the Holland house and already burning from the gazes of passing trick-or-treaters. Two girls from her class, who had both opted for colourful costumes as post-Soviet Russian sex workers, stared at her, open-mouthed as she crossed the road in front of them. 'That's Maddy Matheson,' said one incredulous outfit of squeaking vinyl. Her friend snorted and hit her lightly. 'No it's not. She's like, really Christian. She's no allowed to do Hallowe'en because her dad's like, this insane priest or something.'

'It *is* Maddy, I'm telling you,' her friend muttered. The question was settled when they all turned in to the Hollands' driveway.

'It is you,' squeaked the vinyl. Maddy gave a generous, satisfied smile. 'I thought you weren't, you know, allowed to do ... fun stuff.'

Madeleine was released from having to explain herself by the appearance of Isabella, who created such a vocal explosion at the sight of her friend that the entire party stopped. The teenagers drew in the sight of Maddy like opium smokers sucking the dreamy vapour, and inspected the daughter of a minister who had once prosecuted a colleague for heresy. Lovely Maddy Matheson, the youngest child of a blue-eyed religious fanatic who refused to light a Jack O'Lantern, to hand out sweets to sticky-faced, bucket-wielding hopefuls, and who called most of the internet 'the accoutrements of sin'.

As her father entered the city limits, he turned over the cassette in the car and fast-forwarded the tape to Leviticus. As he drove through the outer suburbs he joined Sir Alec Guinness in a sonorous condemnation of idols, blasphemers, and those who pruned their vineyards for a seventh year. He pointed an admonitory finger at the grinning pumpkins and reminded the plastic witch gaffer-taped to the traffic lights that she was not to be suffered to live. When he and his neighbours (figurative neighbours - the actual neighbours were Vietnamese Buddhists who thought the Reverend Matheson a harmless lunatic) stoned her, her blood would be on her own head.

Her mother watched the evening news and bicamerally mourned the world's sinfulness while wondering what her daughter was doing.

Meanwhile, Madeleine had finally been released from the gaze of the crowd. She was dancing by the swimming pool with the boys from the first fifteen in a cluster which would have sent her father catatonic. She had never imagined that being stared at, as her father once put it from the pulpit 'soaked in the saliva of the eyes of many,' could be so much fun. She had always known that she was beautiful, but she had known it in the way that people with sensitive teeth know to avoid ice cream, or those who get carsick talk instead of reading. She knew her beauty as a minor physical fact which simply had to be worked around. You can know things and not understand them.

Twisting and weaving among the forest of boys, whose desire and tenuous self-control was like ambient radiation, Madeleine understood her beauty. Understanding means knowing the mechanics of a thing, the intention behind its being, the purposes to which it tends, and the capacities of its action.

Several disgusted female guests from the party were making a similar point about Maddy Matheson's beauty, though in less abstruse language, and they left early. And it was simply bad luck that Reverend Matheson caught part of their conversation as he stopped at the same traffic light where, an hour earlier, his youngest child had crossed.

His happiness at arriving home early, to surprise his wife and children in the last restful hours of the sabbath evaporated. He indicated left and made swiftly for the Holland house. Signs along the length of the street promised a *Wikked* (sic) *Partay with DJ Sami-T.*

The Reverend was parking the car in a disabled spot as the prop forward of the First XV, a boy so redolent of sin that breathing apparatus was required around him, handed Madeleine a candy apple with a look of great hope. Fascinated by its glazed, sticky round red wrongness, Maddy took it and licked delicately at the candy coating, watching the boy watching her as she did so.

The prop forward nearly swooned as her tongue touched the shell of sugar, and she wondered if this was the reaction her father had feared, the reason behind his stern stance on apples for the first sixteen years of her life.

Her eyes locked on the boy, Madeleine retracted her tongue from the fruit and sank her teeth, up to the nose, in its flesh. Something sweet and wet dripped to the ground.

At the same moment that Madeleine broke the apple's virginal skin, her father stood seven feet away, scanning the crowd of leering, yelling acolytes from the Pit and wondering where his daughter was. He thought of the papist tradition of Christ harrowing hell; the pagans' Orpheus bringing out Eurydice, even Gilgamesh, facing the underworld for his friend. Fuelling his frustration at Madeleine's behaviour was the Reformation's lack of a literary model in which to cast the problem.

Infuriated by the literary paucity of Protestanism – and remembering Milton too late – he bellowed Madeleine's name.

The party stilled, the guests turned, the First XV broke their scrum. In their midst, a creature uncurled itself and coiled sinuously to face its father.

Her mother's green nylons, seven years of sewing lessons, and a palette of cerulean eyeshadow had culminated in the Serpent itself. Glittering with translucent scales, the nylon skin crept along every undulating inch of his daughter, begging to be sloughed off. Her hair, never before hidden under anything less maidenly than a hand-knitted pompom hat, had vanished under a layer of green gel, which melded with the scales drawn delicately on her face.

Most hideous of all were the ophidian eyes, slit-pupilled and yellow as madness, which regarded him. The rational aspect of her father shouted that it was novelty contact lenses. The irrational aspect wanted to convert to papism and beseech the Virgin for succour.

He looked at her, wondering dumbly at the thing which twitched and uncoiled in the core of his own being, at the snake maiden before him. In the long, expectant silence he registered somehow that this, horrid amalgam of his child with Evil, held a glazed apple in token of her absolute fall.

Around him, the devils began to titter. A wave of embarrassed laughter and pointing fingers began behind the swimming pool of burning fire. One of the lesser demons tugged at his sleeve. 'Come on, Mr Matheson, maybe you should, like, go, yeah? Maddy'll come home in a bit, promise. It's just some fun. No one's bent or nothing.' He brushed the demon away without taking his eyes off the snake maiden, under whose flat scaled belly and roiling hips his daughter was imprisoned. 'Dude, that's just gross,' the prop forward said. 'Leering at your own kid like that.' The laughter erupted into a gale of derision.

The Reverend Matheson came to himself. He considered his ambivalent reaction to this outrage of filial virtue, and fled.

Pillow

Boyd climbed the stairs to Pillow's place, afraid. He understood that being sent to Pillow with Mr Gantry's message was a mark of trust. He also knew that it was a subtle test. Could he deal with Pillow, man to man, on his own, without the backup of Griggs or Ahmed or Donny?

Pillow lived in a nice place. Artsy, but nice. Peaceful. Boyd was surprised. He hadn't known what to expect but the pared-back industrial chic of the warehouse surprised him. It wasn't as if estate agents described houses as perfect contract-killer dwelling, but Boyd couldn't imagine Mr Gantry's problem-solver living with potted geraniums on the stairway window sill, or the black and white photos hanging from the whitewashed brick. He stopped to look at a few. They were signed Bogdan Vic-something-ovic. Was that Pillow's real name? Did he take the photos? A discomfiting thought occurred to Boyd. Was Pillow gay? Was it even possible for a gay man to be a contract killer? He could understand a link between between being queer and a photographer, and even a photographer and a killer, but a queer killer jarred. Fags were all about feelings, and dance music, and the gym.

Boyd looked out of the stairwell window. The building was what remained of a foundry, the office part demolished and only the workshop left in two acres of industrial wasteland. Pillow probably owned it. Where the weeds and rubble ended Docklands high rise began. The plate-glass palaces of tech firms, enablers, facilitators, and lower-grade banker boys who hadn't made it to the City, cropped quietly at the boundary of Pillow's block. It must be worth a fortune, Boyd thought.

At the top of the stairwell a door of caramel-coloured wood had been let into the wall. Four strips of opaque class in horizontal lines matched the same vibe as the photos. Boyd looked up and around.

No cameras gazed down. There was no spyhole, no doorbell. He stood, feeling sweaty and foolish, then knocked hard on the door.

The sound of footsteps, from a light man, Boyd thought. Quick on his feet, smaller than me. He shot his cuffs and straightened his neck.

Pillow was a few inches below Boyd's own stocky six feet four. Slender, but with a kind of wiry, capable strength. Chestnut hair fell back from a wide forehead and matched a thin goatee. Boyd normally hated goatees but Pillow wore his without the usual prissiness that Boyd associated with them.

Pillow looked at Boyd without emotion. 'From Mr Gantry?'

' 'S right. Got a message.'

Pillow turned around and walked down the hallway. 'Come in then.'

Boyd shut the door and followed him. The hall opened into a huge square space, with an artsy looking gallery forty feet up. Windows from ceiling to gallery, then more from gallery to pitched pine roof let in a wan east London light. Pillow stationed himself behind a long counter and tinkered with a machine. A grinding noise and the smell of coffee beans wafted to Boyd. 'So what's the message?'

Boyd, still dithering between Pillow's putative queerness, his occupation, and his sense of interior design, fumbled mentally. 'Mr Gantry's got a problem that needs cleared up on Friday night at Chinawhite.'

Pillow rested his hands on the counter. 'That's a bit public.'

'Mr Gantry wants to make a point.'

'And what's the nature of this problem?'

Boyd thought about her. 'About 5'10". Blonde. Russian. Belongs to one of Mr Gantry's competitors in Georgia. He says to say that you worked with her recently.'

'Ah.' Pillow looked into the corner for a minute. 'Wait here.' He disappeared through a door.

Boyd stood at the counter, trying to take in as little of Pillow's place as he could. He didn't mind working for Mr Gantry. It was better than coffin polishing in Dagenham, which had been the only option after school, but he felt that cultivating a stolid ignorance of what and whom he saw during his working hours was judicious.

All he really knew about Pillow was that Mr Gantry was conspicuously polite to, and about, him, and that he wasn't called in until situations became insoluble by other means. And that he had acquired his professional moniker by smothering two problems at the beginning of his career.

Pillow returned. He showed Boyd a large, high gloss photograph. Wearing a burqa and impossible amounts of kohl around blue eyes, was Mr Gantry's problem. She stood on a street corner somewhere, Boyd judged, in Mayfair. In the background were two black cars with diplomatic plates. Despite the heavy burqa it was somehow clear that she wore nothing under it. One pointed patent black stiletto peeped out from the bottom.

'This the problem?'

Boyd nodded. Pillow put down the photo. 'Tell him the problem will be solved by Saturday.'

Boyd let himself out. He didn't look at the photos on the way down.

Last Round

Allan was playing Banks when I came in twenty minutes ago. So far I've heard *Gimme*, *Trainwreck*, *Beggin' for Thread*, *Drowning*, and *Brain*. I'll go out when she's sung *Contaminated*. I'm not without a sense of humour.

He held up a lime wedge in a pair of perfectly polished tongs and told me it was the last one. 'The last lime wedge in Oxfordshire,' he said. 'Don't treat it lightly.'

The army blocked off the A40 and A34 three weeks ago. It seems unlikely that they'll lift the barricade for a lime to go in my gin and tonic. Not that I'll need one tomorrow.

The sun was on Magdalen tower when I sat down. It glowed for five minutes, then a cloud passed over. The tower makes a good focal point to avoid looking at the street. From the front window of The Cape of Good Hope you can look straight down the High and see Magdalen Tower on your right, and the tip of that weird cupola thing over the front door at Schools. At ground level there's just Roamers, staggering around the barricade on the bridge that separates the hot zone from the outer ring. It could be the last day of Finals, with undergraduates staggering out of Schools into waiting groups of friends filling Merton Street with confetti, shaving foam, bits of octopus, a thousand trodden red carnations. The colleges were always keen to get the finalists to disperse, so that the town council wouldn't fine them for wrecking Merton Street.

Now the Roamers ones can't leave the centre of town. From Magdalen Bridge on one side to Hythe Bridge on the other, Observatory Road to the north and Folly Bridge to the south. A thousand years of study turned into a corral for the undead. When it started I remember a kid saying that no one in Oxford would notice: everyone looked half dead anyway, shambled around demanding brains, and occasionally took chunks out of each other. If the rest of the world wanted to call them zombies, that was fine: within the Oxford ring-road it was fairly normal behaviour.

We're still getting through Allan's collection of strong-woman songs. I suppose it's better than the artificially-generated Korean pixies that passed for music before the world shut down. Nobody wants to die to BlackPink. I figure I have maybe another twenty minutes before I have to go. My mouth feels wetter than usual. I don't know if that's part of the turning, or just because I'm sucking on the Last Lime Wedge in Oxfordshire.

I used to sit here at this bow window, which is like the great cabin on an old sailing ship, and wait for Sean to pass by on his way into town. Sometimes he'd fox me and drive. Either way, I had a combat soldier's sensitivity for his otter-sleek dark head, his slightly rushing gait, or the dark blue VW golf circling The Plain roundabout from Iffley Road. Sometimes I followed him into town. Sometimes I just stayed at the window until he came back over the bridge to Jackdaw Lane and the gym.

Every Saturday. Every Sunday. When he went away on holiday time stopped. I was thrown back on the thesis I was at Oxford to write. Without friends, family, sun, heat, food, or comfort, he – a three weekend stand that got its hooks into me like a yeast infection – was my entire world. It shows how easily-achieved an Oxford humanities doctorate is, if it can be knocked off while servicing a full-blown obsession with a complementary eating-disorder, insomnia, and stalking. Poor bastard, he knew what I was doing and it was – I was – a blight on his otherwise tranquil life. He shuttled between the gym on Iffley Road and his work as a security guard at the Mini plant in Cowley. In between times he avoided me.

When the lockdown happened we were trapped in Oxford – I don't know why he didn't head north to his family, but I stayed because of him. He must have thought it was the End of Days. Not because of the hordes of ravening deadheads who had been infected by a senior fellow from St John's (who brought it back from MOD

Porton Down). No, because he was now trapped in a small town with me: beady-eyed, lissom and reproachful, popping up by horrible chance wherever he happened to be. He loathed me. I loathed myself, in my saner moments. I've taken measures to end those, though.

Then a week ago, the army pulled out and announced they would do perimeter maintenance only, leaving the sweeping to the spill-and-kill groups who were armed, bored, and wanted things to go back to normal.

Pete, Allan's brother, said something that changed it all for me. He was wiping the bar, talking to me and his girlfriend, Patty. We were arguing about whether the infected actually had any memory. Pete said they didn't. Patty was arguing that they showed preferences informed by habit, and that was basically the same thing as memory. 'You see some of them go up the same stair at the same time every morning. Same door, same knock, same handle. It's locked and their tutor's dead, but the habit's ingrained. 11am tutorial, up you go. It's locked into the muscles.' Pete, who was a townie, snorted.

I thought about it. Following Sean around this small town, the same streets, same buildings, same shadows at the same time of day, had become a muscle memory for me. When I needed to memorize something, I used his route from Jackdaw Lane to Magdalen Place the same way Simonides had memorized the guests at a disastrous dinner party two millenia ago.

How nice it would be, I thought, to give yourself up to that muscle memory. The comfort of a well-worn routine, pointless but habitual, without the sense of failure that accompanies consciousness of your own pathetic obsession. Just to be a shambling collection of instinctive, obsessive behaviours. It is the sense of yourself, usually grossly inflated, that makes your behaviour a torment. *You have a PhD,* you think, *soon you'll have two. You're pretty. You're better than this compulsion to walk the same streets looking hopelessly for the same car, the same man. You're meant to be more, to do more. Go out and get him, properly. And if he's stupid enough to reject you, walk away. Let it go and save your dignity.*

Instead, you settle for a sad halfway-house. You sit at a window, waiting to see him. You walk the same circuit so that you'll bump into him. You put up with the same looks of surprise, impatience, frustration, and finally dislike. You wrecked your chances with him ages ago, but now you have something more stable and durable – the ironclad routine of stalking him. The thing that ruins it, as it has ruined so much, is the dreary consciousness that you should be doing something else, that this (actually quite comforting) compulsion is demeaning, unhealthy and (God forbid) unproductive. What would be so bad about being turned? The tormenting hunger for neural tissue? You're used to living with hunger. At some point, before you met him, you decided to live on 900 calories a day. You couldn't control anything else about life in Oxford, but you could show your body who was boss. You're tinier than you've ever been, faint and erratic, desirable to everyone – certainly to him, at one point, before he decided you were nuts. Now your hunger for him is a cliff edge that you teeter along every waking minute. You've arranged attempts at study, exercise, works and days around him. He is as air to the living, blood to the vampire, brain to the poor sods behind the barrier. Hunger holds no fears for you.

I sat at the window of the Cape for a few weeks, thinking about it. Life becomes much more bearable when you admit the possibility of checking out at any time. I gathered that Sean had joined the hunter-killer patrols that went illegally into the hot zone to do what the army wouldn't. I was glad. It felt as if a hard limit had been put on all of it.

Just after noon today, I went to the barricade on the bridge. A Roamer was standing sadly at the grille, shaking it rhythmically with blue-gray hands. We looked at each other curiously for a moment, then I stuck my arm through before he could scare me off with the roaring. He had barely broken the skin before I yanked my arm back and it was done. I pulled down my sleeve and came in here, to my station at the window.

I can feel it coming on, spreading through my whole system. The world is receding and intensifying all at once. These are the last sentences I'll ever write. In the next quarter hour, I'll be released from that residue of a self-image which has made me so unhappy. The same hunger will propel me without shame now. Cleaner than gin. I've just had the last lime in Oxfordshire. He'll find me and put me out of both our miseries.

Time to go.

Allan, the lime was great.

Ramparts

He met her by the city walls, where the sheep picked and grazed among the stony scrub, and lovers, seeking privacy away from houses and courtyards filled with family, met in the rubble-strewn nooks and crannies. On the other side of the wall date palms threw shadows on the scrub like black javelins. He saw Toubkal in the distance, covered with snow and the last light. She sat in a hollow in the wall, covered by shadow, and he tripped over her, falling and grazing his hand on the small sharp stones which littered the ground.

She was fourteen or fifteen, with vast dark eyes and a small, secretive mouth. He thought of Esther before the great king. He wiped the blood from his palms on a handkerchief. She trembled violently and he saw a sheen of sweat on her cheeks and top lip. He bent down to her but she shied away like a horse, curling into the soft, crumbling stone of the wall.

'Vous êtes malade?' he asked.

He sat down beside her. She smelled of sheep, and sweat impressed on dirty cotton, of spices, and snow. He saw her hand, with its filthy nails and toughened skin, shining golden in the long rays. For a moment he thought how easy it would be to take her hand, to take her home and wash her and dress her and embed himself in her soft heart forever. To keep her behind a lattice and make her wine-dark eyes his own solace and secret joy. He brushed some of the red earth of the Haouz Plain off his knees and tried to believe that power can be exercised without sin.

He gave her the handkerchief and she passed it, shaking, over her face, before handing it back. He gave her a handful of coins. 'Achetez des medicines,' he said, and left.

In Sussex, he listens to the sea on the beach and his wife singing in the next room as she throws sheets on the bed that smells clean and honest and honourable, and he buries his face in the handkerchief, smelling his blood, sheep, cardamom, last light, and snow.

Serial

There were cereals whose names Donald couldn't even pronounce, let alone guess which aspect of nutrition they satisfied. Cartoon characters leapt and gambolled over hundreds of boxes and the colours were beginning to give him a headache.

He chose a box at random. It was called Kix. Underneath Chex and beside Cheerios. The whole thing was like a bizarre anagram. With 28.3g sugar per 50g serving.

Breakfast with Margaret had been porridge with a spoonful of honey and whatever fruit was seasonal. In his forties, when he began to direct the business and spend more than sixty hours a week at it, he realized that he only knew what season it was from what Margaret had put in his porridge.

Now she was gone. She was gone, he told himself, staring at a row of AlphaBits, Cap'n Crunch, Sugar Pops, Sir Grapefellow, Crazy Cow, Rice Honey, Cocoa Puffs, Super Orange Crisp, Freakies, and on and on into a garish vanishing point where sugar swallowed all light, heat, time and space.

Donald sighed and moved on to the health food aisle, where everything was resolutely oatmeal coloured, if not actually oatmeal. Here were more things he didn't recognize. What was quinoa? And amaranth, and kasha? They sounded like the names of queens from an H. Rider Haggard novel.

The problem was choice. It had been simple – too simple, he realised. Once, you had liked someone and thought, 'I choose you'. And settled with that choice, being grateful that it wasn't something else you had to contend with. He had chosen Margaret, and she had chosen porridge, and they had marked the seasons with fruit. It was a poetic thought, and it pleased him. He smiled absently at the wholegrain Israeli couscous. A young mother, trailing a complaining child, saw him smiling at the wholegrains and clutched at her daughter as if he meant harm to both cereal and child. A cereal killer, he thought, and chuckled. I should tell Marian that one.

He realized that he had thought of Marian when once he would have thought of Margaret. He didn't feel guilty, only a little surprised, as though he had mastered something much faster than he had expected. Not, he thought hastily, that sleeping with young women – young widowed women one met at a bereavement support group – was an achievement to be boasted. In fact, this is where it left you, in a strange supermarket eight miles away from where he should be eating breakfast, buying strange cereals because Marian had wanted him dressed and gone before her teenage daughter woke up.

'I'd love you to stay a bit longer,' she said, stuffing one of his arms into the anorak which Margaret had bought at Marks and Spencers, 'but she wouldn't understand, so soon after...you see.'

He had seen. He had assured her that he did have breakfast things at home and plenty to do during the day and then slipped out of their driveway in the Vauxhall Astra Margaret had used to run to and from the Bicester shops. He felt like an elderly lothario in the guise of a vicar.

What was he supposed to do now, with regard to Marian? Neither of them had wanted him to say, as simply as he had to Margaret, 'I choose you'. He had chosen once, been happy with his choice, and accepted matters relatively gracefully when death parted them. He wasn't sure that he understood how things worked now, anyway. There seemed to be a heightened climate in men's and women's relationships – brighter, hotter, faster, more...something. And although younger women seemed to pride themselves in their individuality, in reality they seemed as little different from each other as Kix was to Chex, Krave to Krunchies, and everything else churned out in these dreary synthetic flakes produced by an industry which fed on diabetes and pester-power.

Porridge had been good for him, but Margaret had had her own way of making it. He'd tried, once, and burned it to the bottom of the pot. He ate it anyway, in tears, more because of his frustration at how ignorant he had been of everything she had done for him. He didn't feel that he had enough time now to learn a new way of making an old dish. And slight variations on it – this kasha, for example (which was Bulgarian cracked wheat, he discovered) – would only result in comparisons and dissatisfaction.

Donald pushed his basket along the aisle with his foot, smiling pleasantly at the young mother, who had caught up with him and was still eyeing him narrowly. Bread was in the next aisle, he thought. He believed he'd try an egg.

Survey

He is on the sofa with the laptop, scrolling through the family Facebook page when he sees it. *Help us understand marriage and relationships. Take this survey and go in the draw to win a $50 iTunes voucher.* From the University of North Carolina at Chapel Hill. Emily has taken Michael to pick up Daisy from dancing. There is nothing on TV. He has loaded the dishwasher. He takes the survey.

Are you married or in a long-term partnership (>2 years)?

Emily is 28; he is 47. They have been married for six and a half years. Their partnership, however, is 29 years old.

How did you meet your spouse/partner?

There is a list of options: through friends, at work, while socializing, through social media (including online dating), arranged by family, Other. He selects Other. A box opens. He eyes it for a moment. People have been caught out while doing far less dangerous things. Is it really worth it, he wonders, looking around the quiet living room. He studies the small, sweet signs of his wife and young family, in which three decades of waiting and planning have culminated.

And yet. He wants to tell someone, even if it's just this white radio box, which will probably be discarded from the survey. At work he occasionally designs questionnaires. He knows that the named options are what the surveyor usually wants. Everything else is too hard. The box is only there to keep the 'Other' respondents answering and engaged. The text isn't saved at the end. This would be the best outcome for him.

Once he heard Emily telling Daisy a story about Alexander the Great's barber. The barber discovered that under his famous curls Alexander had horns. The barber was sworn to secrecy, but he found it impossible to live without telling, just once, what he knew. He went to a lonely well, pulled the cover off, and shouted into it, 'Alexander has horns!' Then he put the cover back and went on with his life, unburdened. But the words were caught in the well, and continued to whisper whenever anyone drew water from it. In this way we, drinkers from the common well, know Alexander's secret.

He doesn't feel burdened, he reflects. But it the only story of interest about him and is unshareable without triggering catastrophe. Emily is full of stories - he has made sure of this. He has only one, and he decides that he would like to tell it, just once. He puts his tradesman's fingers to the keyboard and prepares to shout down the well.

*

He sent a hundred irises anonymously to the hospital when she was born. It was not so much territory-marking as a way of making sure that she had some story of mystery and beauty about her birth. When her parents-to-be, Caroline and Matthew, chose the hospital from the three in the area, he got a job as a night-shift cleaner in the maternity ward. From 12.45am to 1.10am he mopped the floor outside the nursery, disinfected the door handles, and cleaned the finger-marks of fathers and small siblings from the viewing window. At 1.10am he mopped the floor inside the nursery, making sure to place a hand on Baby Aspel's plastic crib. He did not touch her, or any part of her swaddling blankets because he did not want a subconscious memory of disinfectant or cleaning cloths connected to her far-future husband.

On the second day, Baby Aspel had a new name card: *Emily*. On the third day she had been removed home with what remained of the irises, by her delighted and overwhelmed parents. He reflected on his choice and saw that it was good.

In all, he was a mostly absent suitor. There was no hanging around school gates, no lurking in parked cars or by playgrounds. He trusted that Matthew and Caroline would make good choices for Emily. This was why he had chosen them, after seeing the care with which they treated their unborn child. He had become aware of them when he was working as a delivery man for the florist. He delivered flowers from Matthew to Caroline with a card that said *For my beautiful wife and daughter-to-be.* Caroline opened the front door and he glimpsed a quiet, neutral-toned, freesia-scented home, the pregnant woman in the soft blue jumper, and a life which he wanted.

It was a far cry from the circumstances of his own conception and parentage. The former had occurred in the carpark of *The Bay Horse*, in boozy sorrow after England's astonishing defeat by Poland in the 1973 World Cup. Any parenting had been sketchy and finally shorted out when his father pushed his mother down a flight of concrete steps to her death during a drunken row. In the succession of foster homes and residential centres which followed, he learned two things. One was how to be unobtrusive, and the other was that conventional routes to marriage and parenthood were risky and mostly unsatisfactory. He decided that his eventual partnership would be built on well-tested choices to which he had made a guiding but discrete contribution.

Thus the night-cleaner's position at Emily's place of birth. Then maintenance with the local council, which allowed him to open and close the community hall where she did ballet, to mop more floors in the primary school where her thickly-painted images of Mummy and Daddy and the dog Tolly hung alongside twenty other indistinguishable acrylic families. It was the idea of future Emily, embodying everything that was good and wholesome and stable, which kept him mopping, locking and unlocking, tidying away evidence of half-eaten lunches, replacing lost items of uniform, correcting minor errors in the homework left in her classroom drawer. He did these small, invisible acts of erasure and recomposure because he knew that a child constantly criticized comes to define themselves against everyone else, and there could not be a happy marriage of two people like that.

He selected the stories that would eventually compose her: *Daddy Longlegs* appeared repeatedly in her classroom drawer until she read it. *Howl's Moving Castle, Summer of My German Soldier, A Night in Constant*

Motion, and others from that list of well-received books with an unacknowledged subtext which a paedophilia-obsessed world had nonetheless managed to miss. He read *Lolita*, finally, and was disgusted and appalled by the protagonist's opportunism and inability to restrain himself, his pathetic susceptibility to the attractions of pre-pubescent girls. He had never found teenage girls, or small girls for that matter, attractive. He had been on the receiving end of their clumsy cruelty too many times, the speed with which they distinguished between themselves and his own institutional, National Health-sponsored self. He consulted his conscience and found that he had only ever loved Emily, before even she was born, loved her to the point where he took the barely-formed daughter of an ordinary suburban couple and from that mundane clay, brought his Emily into being.

With this in mind, he oversaw her choice of friends carefully. He marvelled at the luxury of being able to choose friends. He had had to make do with the other relegands from broken and problem homes, the holes-in-their-jumpers, Woollies-plimsols, unwashed List-D candidates who had joined him in agony on the low wooden benches of school-enforced social dancing and partner games.

Because he needed to steer Emily towards the virtue of a working class husband, her small friend Jemima was removed from the position of influence she had begun to exert. Jemima, golden-ponytailed, pony-owning, Range-Rover-chauffeured Jemima, had been blessed with a mummy and daddy who loved each other as much as copious wealth allowed. When Emily's response to denials became standard at 'But Jemima has one,' he could see that even Matthew and Caroline would welcome Jemima's absence. Thus when Jemima's pony threw her and left her vegetative, everyone in Emily's life was guiltily glad.

He saw to it that Jemima's place was taken by Kristin, the small, dark, difficult child of debt-ridden Oxbridge graduates whose eventual divorce reflected the evils of over-education as much as

Jemima's parents had shown the fragility of wealth as a basis for happiness.

Matthew and Caroline themselves provided the final gloss on Emily's unconscious view of a future husband. They provided ten-year-old Em with a baby sister called Madeleine, whose birth placed a predictable stress on their marriage. Matthew became close to a woman called Sally, and their several attempts at a night away had to be frustrated. Sally herself was injured by falling down a cliff while holidaying with her own husband in the Canary Islands. The near miss convinced Sally that she should live more safely and her flirtation with Matthew ended.

When he returned from Spain, Em was about to begin high school. He committed himself to an increased vigilance as Emily teetered between the person he hoped she would become and a parody of it. Thus he bore with the angry buzz-cut, the dreadful music, parties with too much alcohol and boys whose daring surprised even him, abortive attempts at smoking, at sex, at self-piercing, and the announcements to the diary kept in her hockey kit that she would be a painter, lawyer, hacktivist, potter, and off-grid vegetable grower, each one made with the terrifying finality of adolescence.

At a sixteenth-birthday party he had to drag a boy off her semi-conscious body in an upstairs bedroom. He carried her downstairs, through the swirling red lights of a heaving suburban living room reeking of teen spirit, and out to the car. A girl stumbled down the garden path to him. 'Oi - what the...where you going with her?' Dimly he recognized her friend Kristin, painted up like a Russian tart, fighting the need to vomit over all of them.

'Uber,' he said briefly. 'Some kid was trying to have it off with her upstairs. You should take more care of your friends.' He turned away, the moaning stilettoed bundle in his arms. He had to leave her on her doorstep, after ringing the doorbell. Since Em did not have the Uber app on her phone and none of her friends could remember calling one, the mystery of who saved her was never solved.

Matthew and Caroline however, were incensed. Emily was withdrawn from the local comprehensive and sent to a private day school for her final two years. He was surprised - he was occasionally still surprised by the aggression with which the middle class protected their children - but generally pleased, although the new surroundings made access to Emily, her friends, possessions, and work harder.

He took it philosophically and used the time to improve his economic footing. He calculated that he had five years, six at the outside, before Em had finished the inevitable Arts degree and was husband-ready. He bought a book about shares and began cautiously day trading. He discovered that his long observation of people, their desires and habits and fatal vulnerability to trends, were far more valuable than the basic arithmetic needed to play the market.

He began to work for a few local estate agents doing what was grandly referred to as property maintenance. While Em struggled through her A-levels and first years of uni, he was available night and day to tighten taps, paint ceilings, declog drains and replace gutters. When she finished the three-year Arts degree at nearby Birkbeck - her applications for other places having mysteriously gone astray - he took on another man. She had three relationships, none of which were worrying, while he bought a van on which he put the company name. He developed a five-year plan which culminated in a date marked simply on a private calendar - *Em*.

*

'Daddy, what're you doing?'

Daisy, in the pink ballet leotard which makes her look like a small pigeon, blonde strands from her collapsing bun at electric angles to her head, bounces onto the sofa beside him. Em holds a sleeping Michael, curled against her in his nappy like a whelk in a shell. She smiles at him over the top of their children's heads.

He puts the laptop aside, leaving the survey open. Madness, he knows, but in this moment - the lamplight, his wife coming towards him, his children growing every second of the peaceful evening, it all seems all indestructible. This has been his real gift, this ability to read the stress-tolerance of each moment. Em slides Michael into his arms and sinks on to the sofa. 'What *are* you doing?'

'Facebook survey. Well, some university. Through Facebook. You win a voucher or something if Steve Jobs picks your name out of a hat.'

There is a brief discussion between Daisy and her mother about whether ballerinas really must have baths every night. 'It was about marriage,' he says, although she has already moved on.

'What about marriage?' She turns the television on and looks warily at Michael, still sleeping in his father's arms, lest he wake.

'How we met,' he says.

'What did you say?' she says, channel surfing.

'Just the truth - that I came to tighten the taps in your flat because you had a terrible landlord.'

'You make it sound so mundane,' she says. 'You should have made something up. Given it more mystery.'

He kisses her. 'You don't like mysteries. Neither do people at universities.'

She snorts. 'A university? I doubt they know anything about marriage.' She closes her eyes, at peace in her home, with the husband and children she is pleased and grateful to have achieved before she is even thirty.

Rich

Before he left, Cliff said that Rich was typical of how contradictory my life was. Only an idiot would take in an unhappy cat and expect that the combination of unhappy cat and unhappy woman would produce domestic happiness. He couldn't hack it any more (my unhappiness, not the cat's) and so he was leaving. And so he did.

He wasn't entirely wrong about Rich, who really was a spectacularly miserable animal. He didn't like to be patted, he didn't care whether he was inside and warm or outside and soaked. Either way, he moped around with a look my Scottish mother would have described as girning, occasionally making deep, unhappy sounds and farting. It was as though he had some kind of psycho-bowel connection which made him vent his depression anally.

We had found him in the window of a local pet rescue, sectioned off from the romping happy kittens and the sedate, peace-radiating bunnies. He sat in the corner of his litter tray, lord of the shredded paper, glaring balefully at the passers-by whom he knew would never brave that profound feline pessimism. He was like a psychopomp, bodying forth my own inner grump. I was enchanted.

'He's a bit of a lost cause,' the girl behind the counter warned. 'He's been taken and returned twice in two weeks.' Apparently two very nice families had taken him home on the Friday and returned him on the Monday after he had called down Cain and savaged their toddlers. That sealed it for me. A cat who looked depressed and loathed children would go beautifully in my life.

He *did*, in a way. We were both similarly prickly, fond of being alone, particular about what we ate, and stubbornly resistant to the possibility of being loved as most people understood it. We complained a lot to each other and relaxed by washing. We were happiest asleep. I found that Rich validated all my worst habits just by being there. It was a bit of an ego-trip for me, but death to my already-faltering relationship.

Finally Cliff, resolutely Australian - chirpy, poor of vocabulary but rich in stamina for meeting, smiling, and exclaiming happily - packed his things and left. I enjoyed the solitude for a few weeks. Rich was coming into a burst of late-spring-induced lizard chasing, so there was a bit to do around the house keeping up with the body count.

After about three weeks, the silence in the evening began to wear on my nerves. I tried to deal with it by visiting my father and stepmother and three teenage siblings, but their own healthy, unquestioning coherence made me feel like a failure. I came home and determined to be sufficient unto myself and be validated by Rich.

I should mention that we called him Rich after Richard Johnson, the 'flogging parson' who was the first chaplain to preach a sermon in the colony of New South Wales. The name seemed to fit an animal whose attitude to life was mostly punitive.

It would all be fine, I told myself, as long as I had work, and Rich, and something to read.

Then one morning Rich didn't come in. I usually fed him at 7.30am when I got up, and he was almost always sitting beneath the washing line, looking through the window exactly at eye-level, his gimlety glare confirming that I had been a bad bet as a mother and was trying to starve him. When I let him in, he would feed, wash, tell me loudly how bad the night had been, spit at my cuddles and huffily go to sleep on the clean white tablecloth.

I waited until 8.30 and then went out. I thought about him as I walked up the road, trying not to look at the pot-holed surface, terrified of seeing his body, carelessly rolled to the kerb by a car. I didn't mind - well, I didn't *feel* – Cliff's departure too much. It was consistent with how happy we'd been (not very), and how much companionship I'd felt from him. But I couldn't stand the thought of Rich...no, I couldn't even say it.

I went home at 11.30 and stood on the back step, calling and kissing into the air. I felt embarrassed that my neighbours - child-laden on both sides of the fence, and always surrounded by visiting friends and relatives - would hear my thin and desperate calls. I went back inside before the sound of my own voice, single and unanswered, made me cry.

I did some work and thought how the girl had said he was a lost cause when we found him. She had been trying, tactfully, to tell us not to get attached to a cat who was a law unto himself and who didn't seem that attached to existence on the whole. I'd been an idiot, I thought, and Cliff had been right. Cliff's mother had warned him about me in fairly similar terms.

I sat in the bath at 5pm and cried. Rich's disappearance showed the failure of my own condition, which I'd always felt he mirrored. These convoluted thoughts are what single women who have done too much thinking tend to dream up when soaking in warm water and cheap chardonnay while other people band together over the grim reality of life. I was ready to remake it all. I recalled all the pap advice I'd sneered at in magazines and self-help books and pamphlets from various GPs. Advice about building a Support Network and Getting Out and Managing Your Stress with reflection and Hatha yoga.

As I dragged myself out of the tub I felt exhausted. Who was I kidding? It wasn't in me to do any of those things. I hated them when I was doing them, and felt worse just thinking about it. I was lost, Rich was lost, and the idea that I'd discovered a kindred spirit, something self-contained and untrusting, even a little lonely, in every respect like me - that idea was the most lost of all.

I went to bed and cried and cried. And then, in the wee small hours, when it's dark and the snake of despair stretches itself out and measures itself against you, I cried even harder for gladness when I felt a warm and grumpy paw touch my face.

River Road

At three o'clock, Lily ironed the rose dress she had worn to the school formal, just before she found herself pregnant. At four the heavens opened for an hour, soaking the paddocks, sending the horses plunging and rearing. At five Greg came out of the bathroom, showered and smelling like he used to when they lay on the riverbank after school.

Mrs Richards stuck her head around the door. 'Ah - lovely!' she said, with some satisfaction. 'You're a handsome couple, you pair.'

A lilac evening settled on the wet paddocks as they got into the ute. Lily held the bottle of wine from Mrs Richards. 'All set?' Greg asked her. Shyly, she thought him more handsome than he'd ever been at school, now that he was a father and a working man. She leaned over and kissed just behind his ear, where a curl of damp hair met warm skin. 'You look nice.' She blushed. He'd delivered their baby in the back of the ute, but sometimes he seemed like a map of which she'd only seen the centre. She wondered how long it would take to unfold it and lay it out properly, looking right to its edges, and whether there was an ocean or dragons.

They jolted onto the smoother track, towards the river. She looked at his profile in the falling light, handsome and a little sunburned, but more solid, more thoughtful now. There was already a line around the corner of his mouth, from smiling or frowning, she didn't know. She leaned towards him again and kissed the line carefully, while the ute hit small stones and threw her gently against him. His hands, grained with fine dust and oil, tightened on the wheel.

He'd never said the baby was a mistake, never complained that they'd stuffed everything up. He'd just settled it like a load on his shoulders and kept on, quiet and dignified. He'd talked the Richards into leasing them the shearer's shack, and made sure they had somewhere to live and some money coming in, though it ended dreams of the city and college.

Night fell as they rounded the bend and saw the flood-swollen river, sprawling over the road. Greg turned the highbeams on as the soft plash of water hit the tyres. It was four feet, maybe five, deep. Cutting the road off till the morning.

He backed the ute off the road and turned off the engine. 'That's that,' he said briefly, disappointment in his voice. They looked through the dark, dusty windscreen at the Richards' land. *At least we have the house*, she told herself, *we have each other. We're healthy.* Scrabbling for good things, scraping together an armful of blessings.

They sat in silence. Greg leaned his head against the driver's side window. 'I'm sorry,' he said. 'Should've known the rains'd bring up the river. Sorry, sorry.'

She hadn't cared about dinner in town. She had just wanted to see *people*, streets, a sign to the highway. This was their punishment - cut off like three castaways on a desert island. An inside-out prison, endless space and no one within coo-ee. When she'd been at school she'd always wanted to know *why*. Kept on hounding the facts until she saw the reasons behind them. She gave that up when she saw the fibro shearers shack. There was no higher reason for being there, no big secret meaning. Days of dust and boredom, nights of nothing at all.

Something zipped across the darkness. Shooting stars wandering across the heavens. She took off her shoes and opened the door. He raised his head. 'What're you doing?'

'Come and look,' she said. 'Shooting stars.'

They stood on the road, looking into the night sky, vast and incredible, and thought how they had nearly missed it, sealed into the ute and their own disappointment. He opened the back, where his swag lay for long trips to the other end of the property, and pulled her up into the tray. She stood in the back while he unrolled the swag, then took off her dress and laid it carefully across the passenger seat.

They thanked God the wine was a screw-top, and she wondered if the Space Station, passing over them like a diamond in space, could see her unmatched knickers and nursing bra. The Milky Way hung, huge, and the shooting stars came in incredible numbers, like porpoises dancing among the constellations. They lay in the back, nestled in starlight and each other's warmth and soft, sweet-smelling skin.

This was the meaning, she thought, of the shack at the end of the rutted track. Not a punishment but what all lovers wanted, the privacy of their own island, castaways on the beach of the whole universe.

The Silver Bestiary

Christian was the bane of my existence, even years after she left me for him and my passion for her had died down to a dull roar. I met her on a lawn at the university one day, and one night plucked up the courage to kiss her on the cliff at South Head where, like a compass, we remained tiny and still while around us satellites and limpid stars wheeled over the Pacific. And it was only when I was so irretrievably in love with her that I noticed her constant references to him.

She had a passion for Christian which was like a bite, raw and savage and tearing, and as desperately faithful as the thought of one's own death is to the soul. I disbelieved in his existence, until she appeared after a fortnight's absence with bruises freshly made. I understood the cause of her silent, self-possessed love making to me, her abstracted gaze over my shoulder, and that I was only a tide which carried her from one violent encounter to the next. I gave in when she turned on my demands with fury, and when she refused to let me meet him, or see pictures of the holidays I knew they spent together.

She took the silver I gave her and wore it along with his diamonds, and she loved me as much as I should have wanted, but I knew of him. I came across a photo in her notebook and it showed a silent man who projected the arrogance of absolute command and tamed violence. I understood her attraction, she who, having cowed me, waited for someone more forceful even than herself. And I understood that my paltry passion for her paled beside his desire. I saw in him the genesis of her strangeness, the bleeding point of her unforgiving humor.

She left me eventually, and for two long years I tasted salt. His perfection aged me to the point where I no longer believed he could have existed, any more than a god could have.

I finished university, sat beside her at graduation, and caught her mortar board when we threw them from the steps of the Great Hall.

I opened a jewellery shop and designed my own pieces in silver. We had dinner once a week and I watched the fine nose and mouth and the green eyes over the table and pretended once more they were mine. We never discussed him, and I began to imagine she had forgotten him. But I could never tell and only imagined that time, and other lovers had shaken her awake and dissipated him. She modelled my new collection, a bestiary in silver, and in the weeks before Christmas I was almost busy enough not to hunger for her.

She did not tell me where she would spend Christmas, and I was too proud to ask, and I imagined her in her elegant flat, taking to the tropical heat and her solitude with the same self-possession with which she had once taken me. She took to solitude like water, gliding into it and submerging herself in full view, without a word, without a trace. She reminded me of a strange metal, the design of which was like her writing, of a strange depth and strength and tenor, and I wondered what had formed the metal that was her very being, a seam which neither time nor pressure could crack.

I was closing on Christmas Eve when the door opened and I saw him. There is no point in crafting a climax out of it, because it struck me that we were never destined to acknowledge each other. For myself, I was afraid, ashamed, and half in love with the perfection of the man which was like a toxin in the hot air. He, in turn, seemed to understand that other men recognized him and quailed at him, and he carried this power effortlessly.

He came close, and I saw under the fine shirt the muscles which had bruised her body, which I loved as ineffectually as a leaf. He asked to see a piece which, although the most beautiful of the collection, had not sold well because of its strange design. It was a heavy necklace, almost a collar, of silver bees sucking at a row of enormous pearls, as opalescent as moons. The wings of the bees were of the most delicate craftsmanship. The only thing to dissuade a buyer was the strange stillness of the piece, like a garden in dead heat, and the regularity of the silver bees, all sucking at the pearls' nectar like hummingbirds suckling the moon. Only one used to stillness, and unthreatened by the strange tranquillity of my silver bestiary, would buy it and hang it around a woman's neck. Only a woman of surpassing self-possession would wear so many bees at her neck, and allow them to suck the pearls there without fear of being stung to death in her scented loveliness. Only he could have bought it, and she worn it.

He bought the collar and a bracelet, the partner earrings and a huge brooch which I was only dimly aware of having made. Things she told me about him seemed to appear as I looked. The scar at the base of his neck where she had thrown a plate shard at him, and he had slapped her for it. The determined marks from her ten-year-old teeth at the top of his fountain pen. The fob watch I never saw, kept on a chain in his trouser pocket, strange and delicate and engraved with a gryphon. He looked over the jewels and he said, 'Lovely thing', but I did not know if he referred to the collar, or the neck he would hang it around.

He paid for them all with a card, and I saw his name at last as he left the shop and entered a dark car, and disappeared in the still summer heat to her and the blue evening. And I was left in the hot half dark, more certain than ever of the terrible perfection of her lover, who could not possibly have been real.

I sat in the silver bestiary for a long time, a knight captured by the strangest fairy, and thought that she was like her stories after all. Always a surprise ending.

Waiting Room

The waiting room had huge iron radiators. They looked like the ribs of a dinosaur which had got tired of waiting and keeled over before decomposing. Sean scampered around, pulling scratchy wool-cushioned NHS orange chairs from their places around the wall. Daisy folded her arms and hated him. She didn't feel bad about hating him: she had long ago stopped feeling bad about that. With a proper diagnosis of ADHD and many newspaper confessions by bleak-looking women older and cleverer than she about how much *they* hated their children, it was socially fine to hate him. Besides, he never slowed down enough to notice.

He had found a set of crayons, snapped into bits by some other demented child and dutifully shovelled back into the plastic tub of Very Safe Toys by some other mother. He spilled them onto the blue linoleum. Only the green one, a lovely forest green slim pencil crayon, was whole. Holding it out in front of him like a brand, he toddled over to her and deposited it in her lap. She picked it up and he kicked her, hard and swift, on the front of the shin.

It was impossible to kick him back. Even if she could get hold of him, there were cameras. She wanted to get through this without any more paperwork sticking to her. Thoughtfully she massaged her leg and watched him tearing the back copies of Country House and Vogue Traveller to shreds.

He had blond hair, like his father, grandfather, and uncle. Most of their family had been blond. Blond, blue-eyed, intelligent, patriotic, dutiful, the whole grab-bag of extremely English features which shored up a solid education at Oxford, then the Grenadier guards or the Temple, and a safe seat in the Home Counties with marriage to a minor title for the girls.

It wasn't even her father's fault, though he'd insisted she keep it. Not that, at seven months gone before she'd noticed it (girls who

115

married baronets were thin and enjoyed charity marathons and the county fun run), she could have done much else.

Then Tim got himself killed in Basra and the fable was easier to believe. Brothers can't be lovers, even if they're dead.

She had made up a fable about some boy on her gap year, and when she assured them that he hadn't been black or a drug addict or French, accepting the problem seemed best. Her punishment was being thrown to the NHS, a halved allowance, and bleak rural cottage near Pallinsburn which had previously been leased to one of the estate foresters. She accepted this and retaliated by being quite open about the baby's parentage with the attending nurses and health visitors. Since her parents wouldn't have been caught dead in an NHS hospital, it didn't matter that she had made tabloid fodder of their name.

She turned at the sound of footsteps. 'D'you want something, love? A glass of water? There's a vending machine down the hall if you're hungry.'

'Will it be much longer?'

The girl's ponytail bobbed and ducked like a baby bird. 'I don't think so. Carol's just finishing up now with the last person. She'll be with you soon.' She gave a tight, comforting half-smile and vanished. At least she hadn't used the word *pop*. That had become a feature of NHS client (not patient, or customer, or even subject) discourse since it had all begun four years ago.

Something not quite right with Sean. Perhaps you could both pop into the clinic...

I just want you to pop over to a great neurologist at St Bart's...

Thanks for popping in - now you say Sean's ...oh. Ah...

Offspring of close relations can have all kinds of unusual, I mean, unexpected...but there's a good treatment centre, if you can pop up to...

Hi! So this is Sean! So, little guy, let's pop you up here...

Why don't you pop out, Mum, where we can have a word in the corridor...

There were several words, it turned out. They led to a residential program for mothers and children conceived in difficult, usually

116

appalling, circumstances. She had prepared a story about a fortnight with a school friend in Wiltshire, but her parents didn't call while she was at the program, nor in the two months after it. The program proved unhelpful; Sean reacted to more damaged versions of himself competitively, and the other mothers regarded her background as evidence that RP does not preclude Nature's fuck ups.

She began a series of swirling green lines on the back of a pamphlet about diabetes. The crayon felt smooth and thick with child-grime and the sweet waxy reek of childhood. She drew some green hills and a thin green road leading between them. *There must be a road*, she sang in her head. *There must be a road away from you.*

There would be no going back to Pallinsburn. She would never feel her parents' angular, slightly formal affection. No patting Jack, the donkey in the little field by the wicket gate. No more drinks beneath the chestnut in the drystone wall on hot summers. She was corralled with a leopard cub who hated her and would, eventually, kill her.

Sean had scampered himself to exhaustion. Soon, she knew, a series of piercing screams would announce his tiredness, followed by a searing, vicious chase where she tried to grab him while avoiding his teeth, feet, and nails. Every muscle in her back hurt all the time. She drew a high brick wall in the foreground, between her and the crayon hills.

Tim had had too much of everything. He had burned, meteor-like, with the best of the family's genes and the country's history. He had been so radiantly alive that he could brush off their drunken New Year's screw like sparks from the fire. The accidental run-off from a life lived too hot, too gloriously. How could she have known she'd be burned?

She began to draw a ladder, leaning on the green wall.

Window seat

'See that girl over there?' Adil swatted him with a napkin. 'Don't look *now*. Just wait a - now. Now.' Ender turned and saw her immediately. She was just like the last five Hasip had ordered. Slim-bodied, long-haired, pale-skinned. Pushing a tray up along the counter to the cashier. In a notice-me pair of hot pink shorts and rumpled, sweaty tank-top, he saw arm muscles. Runner's leg muscles, too, that the others hadn't had.

He sucked his teeth. 'She looks fit. Are you sure it's her?' Adil produced his phone and consulted the picture. The same girl, more completely dressed, wheeling her bike with a front basket full of books, away from the circular fence around the library. The Korean had done a good job. Ender wondered if the Korean had met Hasip; the photographer seemed to know what would appeal to him. She had deep-set, thoughtful green eyes. An intelligent face. Hasip liked clever women, though Ender couldn't see that he kept any of them long enough to find out what was between their ears.

'Why her? She looks exactly like the others. They all end up in the dam anyway.'

Adil shrugged. 'Who cares?'

The girl paid for a coffee and sat down at the window. She rummaged in a bag and took out a book, pen, and ruler. In the backpack Ender caught a glimpse of boxing gloves and a skipping rope. 'I'm getting too old for this.'

'It's a thousand Euro, Ender.'

'It's life in a shitty British prison if we get caught. And it only takes one to go wrong. She looks like bad luck.'

'Bad luck how? What are you talking about?' Adil's voice rose. Other men at other tables cast glances their way. They were mostly Bosnians, and a few north Africans. They mainly worked on the line at the car plant, or ran minimally-successful import businesses bringing in food and cigarettes for others like them. They all had women, kids, parents at home who thought they lived like kings in the Eurozone, and knew nothing about the boarding houses on the Cowley Road where they slept in a bunk amid the reek of male loneliness and the tyranny of shiftwork.

Ender sighed. Adil was superstitious. His car was festooned with crap to keep off the evil eye and prevent road accidents, gut ache, whores with the clap, the police. There was never anything to attract good luck, just enough to let them slip by without getting slugged by the bad. It was the pessimism of every migrant to Britain.

'Nothing. Forget it. But if she runs, you can go after her.'

'She's not gonna run. I've watched her coming out of the gym. You can hear the music ten feet away. She's in her own world. We'll do it like last time. You do the bike tyres and I'll grab her. Just don't touch the bike again.'

Ender drained his coffee. Three quid and it was shit too. 'I had to. It was going to scratch the car. Don't boss me.' He got up, looking at her. She was looking out the window, too intently to be daydreaming. Watching for someone, he thought. He wondered who. It occurred to him that she looked unhappy. But they all looked like that, the girls at this fancy university. Pinched, anxious, resentful, harassed. That, of drunk. He didn't care. He just didn't like taking them all the way out to Turkey and then having to dump them in the Seyhan Dam afterwards. He couldn't drink tapwater now without wanting to gag.

'Come and get me at seven,' said Adil. He was on his phone again. He never seemed to put it down, since Hasip had made a deal with the Arabs, who never got tired of pale-skinned girls.

'OK,' said Ender absently. He squeezed between the tables, passing her on the way to the door. Her eyes were still glued to the road. He breathed in as he passed the pocket of air scented with her smell, but smelt nothing. They all ended up exuding the same stench, though, never connecting the cold water of the Seyhan Dam to the

Asian tourist who had taken away everything with a single photo weeks before.

Wrack

The dog found her on the beach, washed up like flotsam between two dripping boulders. She had a thin singlet on, shredded by the surf and cruel shells, and nothing else. Face down, he thought she was dead. The dog was insistent, though, so, unwillingly he felt her neck and found a pulse, thready as a tapeworm.

He carried her up to the house, trying not to look at the shaved and swollen vulva that slept, weak and helpless like all of her, between her watery thighs. Although there had been other women after Julia, he had never really noticed. Looking, hard and long and at ease, invited longing. It was what you did when you were in love, and he could not face that again.

He put her on the couch and tucked a blanket around her. The dog fussed at her elbow, nosing the stripes on her wrist, the bruises indented on her thighs like the marks of a seal matrix. She had been someone's personal letter, signed with a flourish, stamped with a sigil, and cast into the sea without a bottle around her.

He built up the fire some more and poured a whisky, then sat in his chair and looked at her. Before, she had been unconscious. Now she seemed to sleep. He didn't want to call anyone. He was the police chief. He was all the police in Paradise Bay. He knew there had been no missing persons, no coastguard alerts, nothing to make the world tap its foot waiting to hear about her.

Sleeping on his couch, under his blanket, she was as defenceless as a ghost. She had tumbled through the sea and fetched up on his beach, track marks between her toes and all, wearing a rag and the signs of the world he had left.

He was too old for this. He was tired and alone and silent and full of years and regrets. He wanted to sit in his chair, in his house at the end of the bridge, with his whisky and the dog he had inherited from some criminal that he had had to shoot. He watched the water evaporate from her in the lamplight, leaving only a strong smell of the sea, as if as selkie had passed out on his sofa. He dreaded her waking up and talking, moving about in the space of his life, dragging out memories and knocking the dust off them.

He could call Kelly, the police secretary. She had daughters this girl's age. He could turn the whole thing over to her before she even woke up. Kelly would deal with it efficiently, compassionately, and without caring too much.

That was it. He didn't want to care. Like most people who live alone after forty, he experienced a failure of his emotional anti-lock system once he started caring. In between the caring and the action, the wheels spun on and on, he slalomed between sex and silence and selfishness until he crashed. He had a feeling that he had been making a slow, controlled crash with the whisky and the telephone line straight to Julia for the last two years. He didn't want to experience a more precipitous crash.

He thought about it, about the girl asleep, about how good it was for a man of his age to have silence and a fire, whisky and a dog. A job policing a small town where people nodded at him, called him when there was a problem, and didn't call him because there never was one. An hour went by. He admitted to himself that he enjoyed her sleep. The deep, determined rest she was drawing and the absolute silence. If she could be like that, he thought, if she could just stay like that, like an oil lamp of rest gently perfuming the air with sleep. I could manage that.

He moved close to her. A hank of dark hair covered one eye, like a pirate. Around her ear a wet tendril curled, a fiddlehead sworl. Feeling the shade of him, she woke up.

She stared at him for a long time. He watched her explaining the situation to herself in silence and perceive him in ways she could understand. The mass of him, his oaken density and age, the lines of world and weather on his cheek, the thick mustache of a man who wore manhood with dignity and was, at times, defeated by it. She took in the room, the fire, the flags of his college team, the dog bed and the glass of amber by the empty bottle.

He saw her eyes turn inward, feeling for any more recent intrusions to her person, and finding only that the sea had scoured her clean, stripped her bare as wood, and tossed her like wrack onto his beach.

She understood that he couldn't be doing with speech and that all he could give her was the fire and time and peace.

She pulled the blanket over her shoulder and went back to sleep.